I0725587

Deathly Embrace

Cassandra Hawke

All rights reserved.

Copyright © 2017 Cassandra Hawke

All rights reserved.

ISBN-978-1-764 3325-1-4

No portion of this book may be reproduced in any form without written permission from the
publisher or author, except as permitted by U.S. copyright law.

This book is dedicated to Duke (John Wayne) 2006 – 2013. Doris's beloved ginger fur baby.
The author's fiesty muse for Cat. You left paw prints on our hearts that will never fade.

Acknowledgements

ACKNOWLEDGMENTS

Cover art by https://www.selfpubbookcovers.com/kshipley

Edited by Georgina Hatchard

Publishing Assistance by Mary Rose Gudzenovs

Prologue

May 1860

She hurried to place his meal on the table as he walked through the doorway. The girls were already fed, bathed, and in bed. But he didn't sit. He stood at the door, his hands clasped behind his back. He watched her.

His face was twisted into an ugly grimace. "Useless woman," he muttered.

Annie straightened her apron and fussed with her hair. She knew what was coming. William was not averse to using his fists when he was angry. If she could only work out what made him angry then she would stop doing it, but it was never the same thing each time. It seemed to her that just breathing sometimes made him angry.

"Bloody, useless woman... for all your money and blue blood, you can't even give me a son!"

He stalked across the room. His fists clenched at his sides, his mouth turned up into a sneer. Annie stood frozen to the spot as she watched him come closer. There was no point in protesting his accusation or in backing away. Any form of defensiveness only incensed him more. So she waited for him to reach her—waited for him to lay into her with his fists.

He swiped the cutlery and carefully prepared meal from the table. It hit the floor with a crash that splattered food on the wall and all over Annie's skirts. She didn't even look down, too terrified to take her eyes off her husband.

He stalked toward her, his hands behind his back. "Useless. Even a two bit whore from the slums can produce a son, but not you. Useless bitch."

She watched him. The sharp smell of his cologne, his sweat, and the pungent odor of aggressive male smothered her.

"William, we'll have a son—next time."

His face darkened with fury—driven by whatever internal demons troubled his soul. "It doesn't matter anymore, Annie, I have a son. Pretty little widow—Gwenie Sealey—gave birth to my firstborn son, Michael William Dunsford, early this morning."

"A bastard to inherit the Dunsford name..." Annie muttered in disbelief.

His fist hit her square in the nose. It cracked and spouted blood under the brutal force.

"Well, if you'd done your duty, I would've had a legitimate one. I intend to bring the little bastard here for you to raise as your own."

"No. I will not. I'll not raise that whore's son."

"You will do what you're bloody well told, woman!" A mulberry hue rose up his neck and over his face. The veins in his neck and forehead bulged and pulsed.

She stepped back. Her fear sharp and gripping. Blow after blow rained down on her. Even though she covered her head and face with her arms and crouched low there was no escape.

Defeated she curled up in a ball and whimpered. "Stop, William. Please stop."

"Useless woman!" He hauled her upright so he could shove her from him.

Unable to resist the brutal force, she lost her balance and fell back against the hot, cast iron stove. Her head cracked against the sharp corner. The brutal blow made her vision blur and legs sag. She grabbed at him. He stepped away, obviously satisfied he'd cowered her enough for tonight. Then she was alone.

Blackness hovered around the edges of her vision. She fought it. Her two little girls might need her, and it would never do for them to know what their father did to her when he was angry. She had to stay conscious and get cleaned up.

***

He would be gone for a few days beginning tomorrow, as he'd been called up to serve on a jury of an alleged murderer. No jurors would be able to return home until a verdict had been reached. She was glad, for it would give her a small respite to plan the future.

Two nights later, she sat alone by the fire enjoying the solitary time. She didn't miss her husband at all as she contentedly filled her time with needlework, painting, and playing with her children—and making a plan to leave this place.

Footsteps approached. Annie looked up from her reading and icy fear rushed through her. The book slipped from nerveless fingers when she tried to rise from the chair. Even before she could gain her feet, she saw the heavy garden tool and knew the intention of her unannounced visitor. The weapon swept down in a circular motion and thudded against her skull.

She sank to her knees. "Please don't..." Her words died in her throat as the tool smashed onto her skull again. Darkness swept over her and she sank into it and knew no more.

Chapter One

Present day

Paige stuffed the letter into her handbag as she climbed out of the car. It was just over a month since she'd attended the funeral of Sarah Hamilton, and she was sure if her elderly cousin, several generations removed, had left her a small bequest, the executor could've just sent it to her.

Her life was currently in turmoil—a broken relationship, a shock redundancy, and the sudden unexpected sale of the house she had occupied for the last five years. She was not in the mood to be arbitrarily summoned to the Adelaide offices of Ashley, Crane, and Atkins—Solicitors without explanation.

Her five-inch stiletto heels clicked with a staccato ferociousness on the tiled floor of the foyer as she hurried to catch the lift. It left without her, when the only occupant made no attempt to hold the doors open. She sighed as she jabbed the call button. After what seemed like an eternity, the lift returned and carried her up to the plush, well-appointed offices of Ashley, Crane, and Atkins. She was late. Flustered and bothered she followed the receptionist into Mr. Atkins's office.

"Ah, Ms. Reed, glad you could join us. I'm Martin Atkins, the solicitor handling Sarah Hamilton's estate."

She took the proffered hand and barely suppressed a shudder at the damp, loose handclasp. Not caring how it was interpreted she hastily pulled free of the contact.

"May I introduce Mr. Logan Dunsford-Hamilton, your co-beneficiary?" Martin said in a formal tone.

Paige studied the man with interest as he rose with the lithe grace of a big cat out of the leather chair beside her. He'd changed a lot in the intervening years. He towered over her five foot nine, was well built, and ruggedly handsome. He held out his hand. She took it. The grip was cool and firm.

"Ms. Reed and I know each other already. Paige and I were childhood playmates many years ago."

Paige made an effort to smile civilly as a disconcerting flash of rage sliced through her. "Of course, Logan. We used to play together at Cousin Sarah's house."

He grimaced. "And you were always leading me into wild adventures, getting us both into danger and trouble."

'Really, Logan. I think you might be exaggerating just a little." Paige forced a smile to soften the sharpness of her tone.

Logan shook his head. A grim shadow danced across his handsome features. His grin melted into a tightlipped line. "I don't think so."

Tendrils of wariness stirred. She tugged her hand from his grasp.

"You were the elder, and the ring leader, but liked to put the blame on me, the baby. Perhaps you thought I wouldn't get punished as harshly as you." A small shudder slipped over her. She didn't remember any specific incident—only the anger, cruelty, and heartache of that last day.

He cocked his head slightly to one side. The angles of his face sharp and defined. "You really don't remember?"

Her all too familiar defensive wall clunked into place, but she refused to look away. "I really don't remember. I suspect I was too young."

"Ah, but surely you remember your invisible friend, the ghost?"

Another shudder, more defined this time, washed through her.

"Of course, I remember the ghost. She still wafts up and down the passages of the old place as far as I know. It's been a while since I was there," she said. She bristled at his audacity bringing that touchy subject up.

"Are you sure you don't remember my broken leg?"

"No, Logan. I don't." A sudden undercurrent of uneasiness swirled through her. She struggled to keep her bitterness toward this man in check as he persisted in reliving a past she had quashed.

He flashed and almost genuine smile. "Well for everyone's sake I'll let it go, but know this Paige I have not forgotten. I'll never forget."

"Or forgive by the sound of it."

His smile widened. "Maybe. Anyway I assume you're as in the dark about this bequest as I am?"

Paige nodded. "I wasn't expecting anything from Cousin Sarah's estate, and I'm keen to find out what this is all about." She turned to Martin Atkins. "Perhaps we should get on with business."

Martin Atkins nodded as he indicated the tub chair to the left of his desk. Paige tucked her tight, pencil-straight skirt around her backside and sank as gracefully as she could into the spare chair. It was low and deep, and as she tucked her ankles together, she wished she'd worn lower heels.

"Mr. Atkins?" she prompted.

"Yes, well..." He shuffled the papers in front of him and adjusted his glasses. "I've asked you both to attend because I have the privilege of bestowing a joint bequest on you."

Logan stirred in his seat. "I don't understand... Sarah Hamilton was a distant relative, somehow, of my biological parents and I've had no contact since I was about seven."

"Give me a moment, Mr. Dunsford-Hamilton, and I'll explain."

Paige looked at Logan and met the direct, appraising stare from his steely grey eyes with an openly curious one of her own. He made no attempt to hide the fact he'd been studying her, as a woman, as a co-beneficiary and as a tiger snake ready to strike. Her face warmed from the neck up more accustomed to men staring at her with lustful expressions than wariness. Resentment flared.

Martin Atkins leaned forward. "Logan and Paige, your bequest comes from the late Sarah Hamilton, a relative—although I'm not sure how you're related, Logan. Sarah Hamilton was, of course, Paige's cousin several generations removed on her mother's side."

"Yes, my mother and I visited and corresponded with Sarah on an ad hoc basis. I came for the funeral." Paige looked at the man beside her, interested in his reply.

He merely shrugged his shoulders. "My adoptive parents and Sarah Hamilton had a falling out when I was about seven. We never went to the house again, and it was too hard for me, as a kid, to keep up with my dead parents' relatives."

Paige's sense of justice was piqued at his off-hand manner. She dredged her memory. She'd always known he was a distant relative but could not remember how he fitted into the family tree.

"Oh, there is no question of your familial ties. Miss Hamilton was ninety-nine when she passed, and as mentally bright as most people half her age. She'd traced the family tree and had been keeping tabs on you both—all of your lives."

Paige shivered as though something had brushed her skin with a feather light touch, disconcerted to think someone had kept track all these years without revealing their interest.

"Now, the bequest consists of the family property located in the hills. It includes twenty acres of mixed native vegetation, cleared land and an eight-room dwelling. The dwelling is livable, but currently in need of considerable restoration and repair. It's the family home, built around eighteen forty, for The Honorable Anne—she was known as Annie to most—Forbes and Captain William Dunsford on the occasion of their marriage. It was built and tied up in trust for Annie's direct descendants by her guardian and uncle, Captain Harrington Forbes. Apparently, he did not like Annie's choice of husband."

Paige gasped. "The house!" Of all the ironic things, she was to share the house with Logan—the man she'd deeply resented all her life because he had caused the breakup of her family. "Why would she leave the two of us the house? What about other relatives?"

"All other relatives have been taken care of. Sarah Hamilton was a very wealthy woman."

"But she lived in such poor circumstances—genteel poverty, my mother used to say."

Logan cleared his throat with a slight cough. "Are you saying Paige and I are to share ownership of Sarah Hamilton's old family home?"

"Yes, Logan," Martin Atkins confirmed with a touch of impatience.

Logan sounded disgruntled. "Sharing an asset with Paige is both complicated and unpalatable. Besides, I have no use for a rundown house. What would it bring on the current market?"

Fury sparked in Paige at his arbitrary manner. "Hang on a minute. Don't I have a say in this?"

"I didn't need to ask. You always wanted the house. Right or wrong you considered it yours," Logan said.

Paige sat as upright as she could in the leather chair. She glared at Logan. "You arrogant bastard. How dare you make such a glaringly wrong assumption."

He looked faintly chastened at her protest. "Sorry. Perhaps I should've asked, not assumed."

"Enough, you two," Martin grumbled. "The sale of the house is not an option. There are conditions attached to the bequest."

"Conditions? What the hell does this old woman think she's playing at? I don't respond all that well to control, particularly from an unknown dead woman." Logan glared at Martin Atkins.

"Well really, Logan, you should be grateful she's left you anything at all, seeing you've had no contact with her for twenty odd years." Paige was ready to spit more, but bit her tongue because she was feeling a little the same. What was Cousin Sarah up to from the grave?

"The decision to take this bequest, or not, will be up to you—both of you. Sarah Hamilton wants you both to share equally in the house, but a condition of Sarah's bequest is that you live in it, together, for a period of twelve months. After that, you may do whatever you please with your inheritance. She would also be very happy if you restored it to its former glory because she believed it would make a fine family home."

Paige struggled to draw in her next breath. How could Cousin Sarah have done this, knowing how much she resented Logan? Knowing what had happened all those years ago. She struggled to voice her rejection, but Logan beat her to it.

"What? You have to be kidding? I'm not interested in sharing living accommodations with Paige, nor am I looking for a family home.

I've just got rid of the one I had in exchange for a very nice bachelor townhouse in the city center," he grumbled.

Martin looked put out at Logan's response. "No, Logan, I'm not kidding at all. It would be inappropriate for me to do so."

Paige choked down her shock and leaned forward in her chair. "But, Mr. Atkins, the house is ramshackle—it has running water and electricity, but no other mod cons. There's an old chip heater to heat water for the bath, a copper for other hot water, and I know the roof leaks. The house is not livable—well, comfortably anyway."

"I have seen the house so I understand your concerns, Paige," Martin said.

"Well, I don't have the sort of funds it would take to restore it either. Much as I would love to own the old place, I couldn't do it justice. In fact, I don't have any money, as of right now, thanks to my unscrupulous ex-partner cleaning out my bank accounts before he left."

"Poor bastard was probably running for his life," Logan said.

She glared for a brief moment at her co-beneficiary. "If you have something to say then say it. Enough with the innuendo. "

Logan shook his head and turned to Martin Atkins. "I might have the money, but I'm not prepared to live with Paige or put money into the house for her benefit so you can cancel the bequest right now."

"Damn you—you're going to reject the proposal out of hand based on some twisted childhood memory you claim to have. And to suggest I would take your money even if you willingly handed it out? I can stand on my own two feet, thank you very much." The sting of tears was almost her undoing. She'd come today expecting a small token in memory of Sarah, not a huge dilemma that included a rundown house, a distant relative with attitude and the stirring of long buried pain she didn't want to face.

"It's not twisted and as I value my life I'm rejecting the offer."

Martin Atkins held up his hand. "Stop—both of you. Paige, Logan, your benefactor, Miss Sarah Hamilton, knew exactly where you both were and what you were up to in your lives. I saw her less than a week before she passed, and she was well pleased with the arrangement. She saw no reason you two could not take up the inheritance, conditions and all. I don't know what you issue is Logan but Sarah gave me no indication the arrangements would be a problem.

"No she wouldn't—she didn't twenty years ago so why begin now."

"Get over it Logan we were just a couple of kids."

He glared. "All right for you. You weren't on the receiving end."

"Enough you two. Do I continue or close the file right now. My time is valuable. As far as I'm concerned it would be foolish to reject the bequest out of hand."

Paige startled at the lawyers biting tone. She turned away from Logan.

"Go ahead Mr. Atkins—we can at least hear you out."

Logan slumped back into his seat and gestured with a wave of his hand that the lawyer should continue.

"She felt they would suit you both—particularly you, Paige, as I believe you've recently been made redundant and the house in which you live is up for sale. I believe you have no wish to purchase the house, so you will actually be looking for new accommodations when it's sold. Why not move to Adelaide? Make a fresh start. And Logan, I believe you've just gone through a difficult divorce and property settlement, which has left you temporarily without anyone to tie you down. I expect your townhouse will be easy to lease to some up and coming young couple."

Logan looked grumpy.

Paige felt like she'd been slapped in the face as heat and color rushed over her skin. "Mr. Atkins, I am somewhat put out you have so little regard for my privacy that you would announce my current predicaments publicly."

"It was not my intention to embarrass either of you. I just wanted to bring it to the attention of both of you that Sarah Hamilton was well informed of your current situations. Now, if you'll let me continue?" Martin glanced from one to the other.

Paige frowned at Logan. He shrugged, but didn't look pleased. A hot pool of resentment ignited in her belly. So much attitude.

"Go ahead, Mr. Atkins."

"In addition to the house, Sarah Hamilton has bestowed five hundred thousand dollars on each of you, to be used as you wish, and another five hundred thousand jointly, to be used for the renovation of the house."

Logan sat forward. "But why do we both have to live in the house—or either of us live in it at all?"

"I have no desire to move to Adelaide, nor to move into the old house with a virtual stranger especially one who has such a misplaced grudge against me."

Martin Atkins shrugged. "That is one of Sarah's conditions."

Logan grinned. "My grudge is justified. Between you and the ghost, a man would be better off playing Russian roulette. "

Paige flinched as a sharp sliver of fear speared through her. Her memories stirred. Warning bells tolled deep inside her mind, behind the locked door. She sat up straighter and glared at Logan. "Don't be ridiculous, Logan. The ghost has always been there and is perfectly harmless."

"You sure about that?" Logan asked softly.

Paige gripped her small clutch purse tightly in her lap. She didn't like where this conversation was going.

"What do you mean—am I sure about that?"

Logan shrugged. "Oh, it's just that you used to blame the ghost for doing things whenever we got into trouble."

"I was a little kid. Of course I was going to blame someone else if it saved me a spanking," she mumbled.

Logan leaned forward, sending the scent of his aftershave wafting towards her. "Martin, what happens if one of us, or both of us, reject the requirements of the bequest?"

"Miss Hamilton was quite specific. If you refuse the conditions of her bequest, the house is to be sold and all her monetary assets split evenly between all the living relatives that can be tracked down. Apparently there are quite a few distant relatives. Both of you would get a share equal to the others." Martin rustled his papers a tad impatiently.

"But why has she chosen us? What makes us special to her?"

Martin Atkins shrugged. "Miss Hamilton had her reasons. She never discussed it with me. Everything is just how she left it, although I did arrange a basic clean right through. The utilities are still connected, and the house is ready for you to move in straight away."

Logan suddenly stood up. "Well, it is a generous bequest, albeit a little strange, but not beyond the realms of imagination, I suppose. It's not like I'm that sickly little boy any more. I suspect I'm more than a match for you now, Paige. What do you think?"

"I don't think you're in any danger, Logan—not then and not now."

"Good then shall we go have a look at our bequest and make a decision whether it's a feasible option or not?"

Glancing up at the handsome man her gangly cousin had grown into she wondered why Cousin Sarah had set up this strange arrangement. She felt as though she was being pushed on a path not of her making or desire. An irrational resistance flooded through her to the idea of living with Logan in Sarah's old house. Deep down she knew it was more than her resentment at what he'd done to her family that drove that desire, but she had no idea why the idea scared her so much.

On the other hand, she was thrilled to have a chance to own the old house. It had always been one of those exciting, slightly terrifying places you went to as a child. It was always dimly lit with bulky, dark polished wood furniture and open fireplaces. Cousin Sarah had baked everything, including the finest sponges, on the temperamental old wood stove. And then, of course, there was the ghost.

Paige groped for missing memories of those years, the house, and the ghost. What Logan had said about danger and trouble sent a shiver down her spine. There was something she needed to remember, but those memories remained as elusive as ever.

"I have seen the house many times, but I never thought to be living in it," she said, as she rose out of the chair with slight difficulty. "It will be a bit like camping out, I imagine."

Logan laughed then, a deep husky chuckle that transformed his face, curving up his wide mouth into an appealing and kissable feature. "I think our erstwhile late relative is up to something—a game only she knows. So, Paige, shall we play or not? That is the question. And what is the price we pay?"

Paige stared up into his smoky grey-blue eyes for a long moment. Mmmm, bedroom eyes were the only way to define them. She considered him carefully before she tore her gaze away. She didn't want to be caught staring with too much interest and give the man ideas. And she wasn't about to admit to herself she recognized the essence of virile male and that her mind and body had responded.

She grinned and kept her tone light. "Why not, Logan? I have nothing to lose. What about you?"

"Nothing of value, I suppose. Except my life." He shrugged and headed for the door.

Again, Paige felt the sliver of unease slide over her. She studied Logan for a minute. Somehow she knew he did have something to lose, but she didn't know what.

"Stop with the insinuations. Either we do this from a clean slate or not at all."

"Okay have it your way Paige. A clean slate until…"

She glared at him. He turned away without finishing his comment.

***

Paige parked behind Logan's red BMW just as he climbed out. He leaned on the bonnet with long legs crossed at the ankles and studied the house. She joined him in that silent appraisal. It was more dilapidated than she remembered. The paint was peeling from the window casings, the corrugated iron roof showed signs of rusting, as did the intricate wrought iron verandah railings. She could also see areas where the sandstone foundations were beginning to crumble. The garden looked dry, over grown and neglected, while the picket gate to the front entrance hung drunkenly on rusted hinges.

She leaned back and looked up the full height of the Norfolk Island pine tree that towered over the house. Its wide spreading branches almost reached the middle of the roof. The gutters were full of the long, prickly, pencil-shaped fronds. After a moment's assessment, she said, "I think the tree should go. What do you think, Logan?"

He smiled down at her, the force of his magnetism drew her in and sent sizzling tingles along every nerve ending.

She retreated mentally from the indefinable shadows deep in his eyes.

"Definitely."

When Martin Atkins arrived, they followed him through the gate and up the front steps. As he unlocked the door Something rubbed against her legs. She looked down. A huge ginger tabby cat wove in and out between her legs. It purred loudly. She bent down and stroked it. It smooched her hand and pressed harder against her legs. She scratched under the cat's chin. "Look, Logan. We've scored a pet cat with the house."

Logan bent down. "Good for keeping the mice down and warming the feet on a cold night." He reached out to pat the cat.

Instantly the cat backed up, arched its spine and fluffed out its fur. The bloodcurdling screech it emitted speared along Paige's spine. The cat suddenly swiped at Logan's hand, with claws extended.

He snatched his hand away and stood up. "Well, maybe not."

Paige stared at the cat, stunned at its sudden transformation. It looked up at her, its golden eyes flashing—the black pupils, just thin oval slits. She shivered as cold fingers of unease crawled over her. The cat had an aura—one that emanated malevolence. Its eyes seemed so full of expression she would have sworn she was looking into human eyes. As she turned away to follow the two men inside, the cat patted her leg and mewed softly.

"Sorry, kitty. He comes with the deal."

The cat stalked down the steps, its tail upright—just the end flicked from side to side.

***

As Logan followed Paige and the solicitor down the passage, he admired the twelve foot ceilings, the wide skirting boards and the intricate cornice. An exquisitely carved arch divided the wide passage into two, adding elegance to the entrance. He remembered a little of the house from his early years, but on seeing it now, he had already begun to fall in love with it.

"The house was built in the eighteen forties, but was modified in the nineteen fifties to bring the toilet inside and update the kitchen and bathroom," Martin advised as he led them through.

"What about structurally?" Logan asked, suddenly interested in the important basics. There was no use sprucing up the surface if the place was in danger of collapse.

"Logan, as far as I'm aware, there are no major structural problems with this property, hidden or otherwise. You can see for yourself there is a lot of work to do, and the sandstone blocks in places will need restoring. It needs re-roofing, amongst other things, and of course, you will need new floor coverings and drapes."

Logan wandered off, leaving Martin and Paige to discuss the soft furnishings for the house. For the first time since receiving his letter, did he truly examine the idea of living in, and restoring, the old house. He could appreciate its heritage beauty, and the thought of restoring it to its former glory suddenly had an appeal he couldn't explain. He had always loved working with his hands and using tools to bring beauty or strength to life in buildings. Long before he had been forced to sacrifice his building company to satisfy his ex-wife's property settlement, he had realized he didn't enjoy the management role the growth of his company had forced him into. This would be a chance to get back to the basics—to get his hands dirty and some sweat on his brow—as he indulged in the process of restoration. He almost laughed; his ex-wife would be horrified.

The one thing that bothered him was Paige. Could he manage her, could she be trusted or would she try to hurt him again. It had all been so long ago. She seemed to have grown up into a normal functioning person. The 'accidents' perpetrated by Paige were burned into his memory. She was the reason he had never returned to this house. He shrugged. I'm a grown man for goodness sake. I'm not that weakling kid anymore.

A soft click behind him sounded loud in the slightly oppressive silence, and he felt the slightest of cool breezes wash past him. He turned. The door to the right was open. If asked, he would have sworn it was shut moments before. He walked through the door and found himself in the very old-fashioned kitchen. It still had the old wood stove with a brick chimney above it. Large, ugly sliding doors hid the contents of the cupboards right along the outer wall. A single sink with old fashioned taps under the narrow, wood-framed, sash-pull window, was the extent of the plumbing. The ceiling was crinkled and smoke stained, and was obviously the original, as it was made with the old, fibrous plaster sheets.

He felt a presence behind him and spun round, eager to find out what Paige thought about taking on the bequest. The room was empty, the door standing open as he'd left it. A shiver danced along his skin. He crossed the room and reached for the door handle. It jerked away from his grasping fingers, and the door slammed shut with a resounding crash.

"Damn," Logan muttered, as he looked around the room again. It was empty. He reached for the handle again, took a firm hold of the handle and opened the door. He slipped through it with a short urgent movement. He shut it with a deliberate gentleness, but as he stepped away, he heard a creak. He looked over his shoulder in time to see the latch lift and the door swing open just a few inches. Obviously something was way out of alignment there, but he was sure it was nothing a good carpenter couldn't fix.

"Paige? Martin?" he called.

"We're in the dining room," Paige yelled back.

"Well, you two, what do you think?"

Logan cast his gaze around the room, taking in the peeling paint and shabby carpet on the floor. "It needs a lot of work." Despite this obvious observation, his enthusiasm for the project was growing by the minute. He was pleased to see the shine of eagerness in Paige's eyes.

"I'd forgotten how beautiful this house was. It would be great to see it restored back to its former glory."

"It would be profitable too," Martin said.

Logan sensed Martin was keen to finalize this estate with Sarah Hamilton's instructions satisfied, and he wondered again what was behind Sarah Hamilton's strange bequest and the binding conditions that came with it. Considering what had happened all those years ago, he was surprised Sarah had made this a joint inheritance. Everyone knew how much Paige wanted the house, even at four years old she had told him he couldn't have it. Logan watched her for a second and wondered how much she actually remembered of the incidents, the consequences, and if she still wanted the house badly enough to repeat her actions. If he accepted this strange arrangement, he could be opening up old wounds, memories, and rivalries that were best left buried. He wasn't even sure how far he could trust Paige. His adoptive parents had claimed she was a psychopath in the making and refused to let him visit after the last incident left him with a broken leg.

Despite the issues, he felt a surge of excitement. In front of him was a beautiful woman who, only hours ago, was nothing more than a vague, uneasy childhood memory, and now his future was tied implicitly to hers. He wanted to accept the gift, conditions and all, and he was suddenly afraid she would refuse to be part of it considering his first response had been negative and accusing. "Paige?" he asked.

She looked up at him. Her soft violet blue eyes sparkled. When she smiled, the fullness of her shapely mouth was a silent invitation to be kissed. "So, you've decided you want to accept now you've seen how beautiful it is?"

He nodded. "It appeals... the work required might soothe my angry soul."

"Angry?"

He laughed then. "You know... a cathartic thing to do. Heal the broken soul and all that."

"Are you sure? The ghost and I come with the deal. I wouldn't like to think you're waiting to be murdered in your bed for the next year."

Logan grinned. "Okay point taken."

A tremendous clatter in the hallway cut off her protest. Both men hurried out into the hall.

Logan came to sudden halt. The umbrella and hat stand lay on its side. The items once hanging on it were scattered across the hallway.

"What the heck?" he blurted out.

Paige came and looked over their shoulders. She laughed, and her eyes sparkled even more with latent mischief. "Oh, that would be my invisible friend, the resident ghost."

Logan looked around at her, not sure if she was joking or not. "Oh, so that is how it is going to be, Paige? Blame the ghost when anything happens?"

Paige stopped laughing. She looked serious. "I'm not a kid anymore, Logan, but there is a ghost in the house, and she does things."

"Really, Paige, give it up, and please don't try to talk me around with mumbo jumbo."

"Oh, I won't bother. Living here will do all that for me," she said with a chuckle.

He didn't like her laughing at him. It reminded him of his wife. She had laughed at him too—at his reluctance to make her a director in his company, to pool all his money in joint accounts, and when he asked about discrepancies in the accounting figures. Goading laughter, loaded with the silent accusation. He didn't love her enough to trust her. Well, he'd trusted her, and look where it had gotten him—broke and broken. No, he didn't like women to laugh at him.He glared at Paige and her laughter faded.

"Yes, Paige, things do happen in this house, but I don't believe they are done by a ghost, either back then or now." He was aware of the dripping sarcasm on his words—far more than the situation warranted.

She looked up at him, her face still and serious. He saw for the first time, fear in her eyes and a tenseness about her body—like she wanted to run. He wondered why? Surely she was not frightened by a touch of sarcasm. Maybe she remembered more of the past than she was telling.

"That sounded like an accusation. I told you, I don't remember what happened when I was four. If you have something to say about it, do it now—or leave it alone." She glared up at him, almost daring him to speak.

"Oh. I wasn't accusing you of anything. I just don't believe in ghosts. That's all. So do we do this?"

She nodded. He saw the doubt in her eyes and guessed it was a reflection of what was in his own. She looked around the room as she took the papers from Martin then without another word signed them. She stepped back from the table.

"You're sure, Paige, before I seal the deal."

"Yes I'm sure, besides we're grown up now."

Logan affixed his sprawling signature to the papers and handed them back to Martin.

With the papers signed, Martin Atkins gave them each a set of keys.

"I expect you to move in within the month, preferably before. I will be keeping tabs on you as demanded by your benefactor. The bequest will only be finalized at the end of the twelve months if you have fulfilled the conditions set out in the papers you have signed. Now, is there anything more you wish from me before we leave?" He guided them out onto the front verandah.

Logan paused at the top of the steps. "Thanks, Martin but I think Paige and I can muddle through."

She nodded, and Martin turned away almost tripping over the cat as it darted between them. In a flash of ginger the cat landed on Logan's chest, dropped to the ground and darted away. Logan yelped as he fell in a slow backward topple. He landed on his backside with a painful thud, slid with three jolting bumps down the remaining steps before crashing onto the garden path. He groaned as pain spiraled up his back.

"Are you all right?" Martin asked.

Logan groaned again and rubbed his back.

Paige touched his shoulder softly. "Do you need help to get up, Logan?"

A shaft of hostility speared through him as he looked up at her. "No, but I might need help staying alive if I move into this damn house with you. I don't know what I was thinking to agree. Actually, I probably wasn't thinking at all."

Paige reared back. "I never touched you."

"No, she didn't, Logan, and I think it's mightily unkind of you to suggest such a thing." Martin's face was red and sweaty. "The cat leaped at you."

Martin held out his hand to help Logan rise, but he ignored the proffered hand and climbed to his feet unaided. He winced as he moved.

He looked from Martin to Paige then across at the cat, now perched on the lone garden bench by the rose garden. "Fine, if you both say so."

"Do you wish to renege on the deal, Logan? Obviously if you think I or the ghost might cause you harm, it might be best."

He smiled. "No, Paige, I do not wish to renege on the deal, but I will be watching you closely from now on. I will not allow any repeats of your childhood pranks."

"Damn you, Logan. I've told you already, I don't remember any pranks."

"Enough, you two. I have to get back to the office. Do we have a deal or not?"

Paige looked at Logan. All the resentment bubbled up, fired by his new accusation.

He glared back at her then turned to Martin. "We have a deal, Mr. Atkins."

Chapter Two

A few days later, Logan moved in. The tension between him and Paige had eased, and he'd made a concerted effort to put the steps incident behind him, along with the ones from their childhood.

It had taken some deciding what to store and what to bring, but between them, they'd eliminated all the double up in furniture and white goods. Along with Sarah Hamilton's old-fashioned stuff, they had put everything they didn't require right now into a large storage shed. They had kept the furniture to a minimum, leaving most of the rooms sparsely furnished or empty ready for renovation.

Logan was glad to have a chance to inspect the place, alone, and decide on what would be done, which was most urgent and which was most costly. As he worked with Paige over the Internet to draw up plans and collate ideas, he'd become more and more enthused about this restoration project. He climbed on the roof and into the roof space, poked and prodded pipes and wires, and made copious notes on tasks to be done—what was needed and who he should get to assist him. He went through each room, one at a time, and drew up plans for changes.

It was obvious the lounge room had not been used in ages and badly needed airing, so he put his paperwork down on the floor and went to unlock the windows. Before he could open them, there was a rattle and a crash behind him. He turned and his heavy notepad caught him squarely in the side of the head. "Ouch," he yelped.

He touched his face, and it came away with a smear of blood. He glanced around the room. All was still and silent. What the hell had caused that? He refused to believe in Paige's ghost. He hadn't as a child, and he certainly didn't as an adult. He shrugged. There must be a simple explanation. Then he saw the cat sitting on the hearth. It was busy cleaning its front paws and wiping its face. It paused in its ablutions and hissed at him. He put his hands on his hips and glared at the feline.

"So, was it you, Cat? I gather you don't like me, but you will have to do better than that to scare me off. This is my house, so you can stop the scare tactics right now."

In a blur of orange, the cat pounced. With a flurry of claws and fur, his pencils and rulers whizzed off the floor, and stabbed at his legs and chest with sharp points.

As he fought off the missiles, he shouted at the cat. "Hey, you, enough! This is my house. Get lost."

He waved his hands and made a spitting noise at the cat. It spat back at him before it turned and stalked out of the room, its tail straight in the air, the tip snapping from side to side.

Stillness and silence descended.

"That's better. Get out and stay out, Cat." Logan felt foolish talking to the empty room.

Nothing stirred. He gathered up his materials, opened the windows, and moved to the next room.

By late afternoon he had a long list of work to be done in addition to the big jobs he and Paige had already agreed upon. Tired, but satisfied with his day's activities his thoughts turned to food.

When they had discussed their accommodation arrangements, he'd made it clear, that if she expected him to share cooking duties; he would not be using the wood stove. Fortunately, she agreed wholeheartedly with his suggestion they get a portable gas stove, to supplement their microwave although she did admit to cooking a chocolate cake in the oven once, under Sarah Hamilton's supervision.

With plans to demolish the current kitchen, which was no more than a lined lean-to on the back of the house, they had chosen the room adjacent as a suitable substitute kitchen. The light was mellow, barely reaching the corners of the room and the high ceiling that towered overhead. He lit the small primus and slapped a steak from the fridge onto the grill. He tossed a salad.

The yowling of a cat disturbed the quiet. He looked around, and saw Cat sitting upright on the outside window ledge, running its claws down the glass. Logan stared at the cat. He had no intention of letting the vicious feline in and so he didn't feel guilty refusing it's desire to come in, he pulled the curtains across.

It's smell of filled his nostrils and clogged his throat. He coughed. His head spun, and his vision blurred. He swung around. The flame on the primus stove was out, but the gas continued to hiss. He turned it off then fled outside for some fresh air. The back door slammed shut behind him, so hard the glass in the adjoining window shuddered.

As he wiped the tears from his eyes, he stared at the door. There was no wind outside. It must have been a draft in the house or that wretched cat. He felt in his pockets. Damn, the keys were on the dining room table, as was his mobile. Frustration flared—he was hungry, tired, cold and now locked outside in bare feet.

Then he remembered the windows he'd opened earlier. Probably a breeze wafting through had blown the door shut, but they were also his way back into the house. He struggled to find his way around the side of the house in the dark, through the over-grown garden, and along the crumbling concrete path. Stabbing pain shot across his foot and up his leg. "Owwww." He peered down. It was too dark to see the damage to his big toe, but he felt the slippery moisture between his toes. He hobbled. Stones stabbed into his soles and he hopped from one foot to the other. Damn damn damn. Note to: self carry keys, get a torch and suck it up. He sensed rather than saw the branches hanging low by the corner of the house and ducked. The foliage brushed his hair. Two more steps jiggling steps before he reached the first window.

His hand touched the sill. Peeling paint crackled, and the timber creaked. He snatched his hand away as the window dropped down and slammed shut. The ledge trembled. The faint reflection of the moonlight in the glass shimmied. The glass creaked. Logan bucked back. His heart pounded. "What the fuck?" A cat howled. Unease raced in cold fingers over his skin.

He pushed it away and turned to the second window of the pair. He looked at the timber and glass pane suspended above him. It seemed solid. He slapped his hands on the frame and hiked his leg over the sill. He straddled the opening. The timber creaked. The window sash jerked and snapped against the frame. Logan lunged into the room. The heavy bottom rail of the window crashed hard across his backside and scraped the full length of his thigh as he slid through the opening and thudded onto the floor. The window slammed shut. The glass rattled in between the sash bars.

Even with the heavy drapes drawn full open, it was almost completely dark inside. His back throbbed and his leg stung. He guessed he would be bruised and sore tomorrow. He lay for a while on the floor, absorbing his pain. God that hurt. He looked up at the windows. Well can't blame Paige for that one.

His mind drifted back to the first incident involving him and three-year-old Paige. He'd been left to wait in his parents' car as they said farewell to Sarah. Paige had been by the driver's door blowing him kisses. The next thing he knew, he was alone in the car, and it was rolling down the driveway. His father and Paige's had dashed after the car, but neither reached it by the time it veered off the driveway and into the gatepost. He'd been shook up, but not hurt. His father had berated him about touching the mechanics of the car, even though he'd vigorously denied doing anything. Malcolm had blamed his own daughter, but when questioned, Paige had blamed the ghost. Sarah and Paige's mother, Jane, had laughed it off, and Sarah delicately suggested that his father, David, had not put the hand brake on sufficiently.

He shook his head. No I can't blame Paige this time.

With a groan he climbed to his knees and crawled with painful caution across the room. He was going to need a wall to get up. A spasm of pain stabbed down his back and thigh. His big toe throbbed and stung. He reached for the door jamb and levered himself up. A movement. The tiniest change in the darkness. He swung his head around. Lost balance. Grabbed the door and steadied himself. He probed the gloom, squinting his eyes to see better. A shimmer against the shadows. A swirl of grey mist. He gulped. His heart leaped then pounded in an erratic rhythm. A woman ethereal, translucent—tall and willowy, with long curls done up under a delicate lace cap. Unease shivered along his skin. The hairs on his arms rose. What the fuck?

He recognized the face—its delicate beauty, high cheekbones, and soft strawberry curls—Paige.

"Paige?" he asked. There was no answer. "Come on, Paige, this joke has gone far enough." Irritation flared. "It's not going to work, you know. There are no such things as ghosts. Give it up, Paige." Irritation transformed to anger. "Enough."

The vision did not answer. Her skirts were full and long. She appeared to float along the floor. Cat wove in and out of her rippling hemline. The shape undulated. A hand rose. A finger pointed in the direction of the window. A whisper filled his ears. "Get out of my house. Go now or die."

Indignation exploded. "No damn you I won't. So stop bloody well playing games, Paige."

A tinkle of laughter danced through his head. Then the vision faded. Darkness and silence descended. Only Cat remained in the middle of the floor. Logan reached for the door handle. It was cold—so cold it almost burned his palm as he struggled to turn it. With the slightest of clicks, the lock released and the door swung open. The passage beyond was empty.

"Damn it, Paige. That was not funny," he grumbled as he reached up to turn the light on. No-one was there. His face suddenly warmed as he turned on his heel and stalked to the kitchen, feeling like a right twit. *Let yourself get right spooked didn't you.*

He shrugged as he re-lit the stove. *Stupid, stupid, stupid.* "Drafts, crumbling window panes, and a feral cat—dangerous place this old house, but there are no such things as ghosts."

He ate then still uneasy made a quick inspection around the house. He was totally alone. Even Cat had gone. Logan made himself comfortable for the night in the front room he'd chosen for his bedroom. It took a long time for him to settle, as the shadows in the room appeared to move and drift. His thoughts were a jumbled and confusing mixture from childhood and now. He liked Paige, but could he trust her? At last he closed his eyes...

***

He saw her coming towards him, her long flowing nightgown billowing around her as she glided across the room. Tall and willowy, he could just make out the curves of her naked flesh through the translucent material. Her full, rounded breasts undulated slightly with her movement. Large nipples, dark and erect, pushed against the restraining folds of fabric. Her luxuriant strawberry blonde tresses hung almost to her hips. Soft curls danced over her shoulders and almost hid the deep cleavage that pushed up above the low, lace-trimmed neckline of her gown. The creamy mounds of her breasts cried out to be caressed. He licked his lips. His cock stirred. Desire tightened his balls.

It had been a while since he'd had a woman in his bed and never one so enchanting as this vision before him. He could smell her scent now, a delicate, old-fashioned rose perfume, underlying the intoxicating fragrance of a sexually aroused woman. She smiled at him, the full lips parted to show small white teeth. The tip of her tongue slid along the plumpness of her bottom lip.

His stomach clenched and his cock hardened, pulling his balls up with it. She held her hands out to him, and he flicked back the blankets to reveal his arousal and invite her to join him. Her hands fiddled with the ribbons at the neckline of her gown. As they loosened, she slipped the gown off her shoulders and let it fall in a fluff of white cloud at her feet. She was stunning—smooth white skin, full breasts, slightly rounded stomach, and gently curving hips. Her long legs ended in small, bare feet. At the apex of her legs was a tangled bush of strawberry blonde pubic hair, slightly darker than the hair on her head, which fully covered the generous mound of her outer lips. His hand itched to slide through that bushiness and explore her hidden recesses.

Her skin was cool and smooth against his as she slid in beside him. He reached for her breasts, but she pushed him back until he was lying flat against the pillows. She flicked the blankets off the bed fully exposing his naked lust. His cock was rock hard, throbbing, the exposed head already damp. She leaned down and kissed his lips with the lightest of touches before her mouth moved along his jaw, down his neck and onto his chest, nibbling and kissing.

He stirred restlessly on the sheet. He put his hand down and cupped his balls, pressing them gently to ease the aching tightness, before he slid his hand up his shaft. She pushed his hand away then went back to kissing and nibbling a fiery trail over his chest and abdomen. She paused at his navel to dip her tongue into the large, shallow indentation. He shivered as she slid her moist tongue in and out in a staccato rhythm, to simulate thrusting. Then she pressed her tongue into the deepest bit before licking the rim and moving on.

With a moan he lifted his hips toward her. He tried to touch her breasts, but she pushed his hands away, and she kept her legs tightly together, so even when he reached between them, he could not gain access. His every nerve ending jumped with erotic awareness. His cock ached with the need to be stroked and touched, and all he wanted to do was push her down on the bed and bury his throbbing organ in her hot, wet pussy. Somehow, she held him inert on the bed with just a stroke of the hand or a gentle push.

He felt powerless to argue. "Touch me... please put me out of my agony," he begged, and lifted his hips until the tip of his cock just slid against her arm.

She laughed now. A melodic tinkle that was both beautiful and spine tingling.

He was taken aback by the sound and his cock danced a little as his desire faded for the briefest of moments, while he tried to reconcile his thoughts and his desire.

Her laughter had barely faded when she dipped her head. He nearly screamed with pleasure as her tongue flicked swiftly back and forth over his head, tasting and spreading the moisture leaking from his tip. Then her mouth enveloped his cock, sliding with tormenting slowness down his shaft until she had taken all his thickness and length into her mouth.

"Oh my God," he cried out, as he squirmed with the ecstasy of her mouth as it slid up and down his shaft, and her tongue flicked lightly over and around. He moaned. She sucked deep again and at the same time, she brought her hand up to cup his balls, kneading gently before rolling each testicle around in the wrinkled skin covering. "I'm going to explode... that's so good," he moaned.

He raised his hips to thrust into her mouth, but she pulled away and sat up straighter beside him. He watched her. She looked deeply into his eyes. He stared back until he could feel himself slipping into her stare, drowning in the azure blue depths. He didn't feel love. She wasn't smiling, but his body was overwhelmed by the agonizing need to possess this woman, to take her, to bury his cock deep in her body. His legs twitched and his hips lifted with his aching need. She lifted herself, and with delicate care, she straddled his thighs. She watched him as she reached out and stroked his cock with her hand. The skin was smooth as satin, but the lack of lubrication heightened the sensation to an almost painful pleasure.

He groaned. "Put me out of my misery. Please... take me."

She stopped stroking and lifted herself over his erection. He could just see the deep pink of her inner lips as she parted her legs then she was sliding down on his shaft—so slowly, so exquisitely slowly. His cock slid easily into her moistened pussy. He felt a delightful tightness enclose his cock. He thrust upwards and pushed his member as deep as he could. She took him all. He held her hips now and thrust fast and hard.

In response she rose and dropped in unison with him. Her hands spread on his chest as she gave herself leverage. She moaned now and gave little whimpers of pleasure. He thrust deeper and slower now. He wanted her to climax, but he didn't know how long he could hold back. His cock throbbed and pulsed. His breath came in small, hurried gasps as his orgasm built. She stilled then, as he kept thrusting, arched her back, and cried out again and again.

He felt her pussy clutch and squeeze his cock through its throes of orgasm. He moved with a desperate rhythm. She cried out again, this time, a nerve tingling howl, as she pushed hard against his upward movement, her nails scraping across his chest. Her pussy grabbed his cock and he exploded. His orgasm roared through him and down his shaft in almost painful undulations that reverberated right through his body. A groan ripped from his chest as he felt his seed spurt out with throb after throb. Then he was spent. He sank back onto the sheets, his eyes closed, his mouth open, as he sucked air into his aching lungs. Sweat popped out on his bare skin as he sank into satiated lethargy. He reached to pull her into his arms as he opened his eyes.

She was gone. There had been no sound of departure, but she was definitely gone. Vague resentment balled in his gut. He looked at his phone. Three in the morning. Maybe he'd been dreaming. He reached down to his cock. It was soft, relaxed, and sticky. So, it wasn't a dream. She'd been here. He'd had sex with a stunningly beautiful, unknown woman who reminded him so strongly of his absent housemate.

He got up and looked through the house. It was deserted. Even the cat was gone. He felt uneasy, but brushed it off as he washed himself clean and went back to bed. He was asleep in a moment, the fuzzy relaxed glow of total sexual satiation cradled him lovingly.

***

The call of the magpies woke him just after dawn and he immediately became aware of a chill in the air. He rolled out of bed and stretched his hands over his head. He noticed the red grazes across his chest—not enough to bleed, but enough to score the surface of his skin. He looked down at them puzzled then shrugged it off—probably from last night's little escapade with the sliding windows. Although he remembered the feel of his dream lover's nails raking his skin, he was not prepared to admit that was the cause of his injuries.

Then he noticed the breeze—the crisp autumn breeze billowed the curtains half way across the room as it came through the open windows—windows that had definitely been shut and locked when he had gone to bed last night. He left them open in his bedroom and went to inspect the rest of the house. Every window and door in the house was open. It had to be Paige. There was no other rational answer.

"Damn you. Quit the funny stuff," he muttered.

Paige must have arranged for this little joke on him, to get him back for his accusations about the past. He wasn't sure how she would have achieved it, but he was sure she was behind the happenings. He suspected she still wanted the house for herself, just like all those years ago. But just scaring him out of the house was not going to get her what she wanted. She would have to kill him. He shook his head to clear his twisted thoughts. Good grief, his parents' paranoia must have really sunk in.

"This is ridiculous," he muttered. He punched Paige's number into his phone. She answered.

"Where are you?"

"Me? I'm on the ferry, just leaving Circular Quay. Why?"

"So how much did it cost you to get the little ghostly jokes carried out? You aren't going to scare me out of the house you know."

"What are you talking about, Logan? What ghostly jokes?"

"Oh the killer windows, the spectral visions, all the open windows."

"What are you talking about? I haven't arranged anything."

"Look, I want to believe you, but strange things have been happening here..."

Paige chuckled down the line. "Strange things like doors opening and things moving?"

Logan frowned at her laughter. "Yes."

"Well, don't worry. It's only the ghost. She doesn't like you."

"There are no such things as ghosts. There's got to be a logical explanation..." He shook his head.

"Well it wasn't me so I suggest you be nice to her, or she might hurt you. See you soon."

She was gone. He looked at his phone. He felt foolish now. Practically accused her of messing with him, and it was obvious she was in Sydney. Besides, he didn't really think she would stoop to such tactics to prove a point. *I need a strong coffee. Clear my damn head.* He headed for the kitchen.

Cat was waiting for him. He gave him a saucer of milk.

"Killer's spawn." It was a breathy, sobbing whisper that went on and on. It seemed to be in every room. It swirled around him, bombarding him from every side.

Logan covered his ears. "Not listening." A shiver ran over his skin. With rigid determined movement he made a coffee, snatched up a couple of Tim Tams and went out into the sunshine.

He had always treated the paranormal with blunt skepticism. But now as he went over the incidents, he began to wonder if there was something going on here that he didn't understand. Regardless he'd enjoyed his 'wet' dream last night. She could come anytime and he'd make her welcome. An hour in the sun, and a couple of hot coffees later, he was ready to laugh again at the thought of ghosts. With his enthusiasm restored, he donned work clothes, and began pulling up the old moth-eaten carpet in the second front room. He was down to the last of the underlay when the commercial sized rubbish bin was delivered.

After a late lunch, Logan made arrangements for a couple of tree loppers to give him quotes. As he didn't care about the cost, he chose the most professional sounding outfit and made arrangements for it to be done. He returned to pull up more carpets, revealing stunning floorboards that just begged to be sanded and polished. He was glad that his practical joker and offsider, Cat, had been quiet all day. It gave him a chance to put some distance between him and his doubts.

***

Tired and grubby, Logan set the fire in the dining room, ordered pizza to be delivered then stripped and headed for the shower. As the hot water sluiced over his body, he toyed with ideas for the bathroom.

The current bathroom was a huge area that could be divided into two smaller bathrooms or a large bathroom with spa and toilet, and a second, separate toilet. He also thought about the laundry, because that was the same size and he wondered if he could turn the adjacent room into the master bedroom and make half the laundry into an additional bathroom.

He soaped himself and shampooed his hair, glad he kept it in a short style these days, as it was easier with the dust and grit that came from building sites to keep it neat.

A resounding crash, echoed loud over the water. He reached for the taps and turned the water off. What the fuck now? God damn this bloody house. He reached out of the steamed up cubicle for his towel, water still streaming down his face. His grasp found air. He swiped the space. Nothing. *Bloody hell. He was sure he had left it on the rather dodgy towel rack*. He groped farther. Something warm and alive touched his hand. He yelped, dashed the remaining moisture from his eyes, and slammed the curtain fully open and leapt out of the shower cubicle. "Who's there? Stop your bloody games. It isn't funny anymore." Sizzling with anger he surveyed the room.

His shaving cream and razor lay on the floor, drowning in his aftershave, leaking from the shattered bottle. He looked for his towel. It was lying in the middle of the puddle of perfumed liquid.

Cat sat on the edge of the basin.

"Damn animal. Cat, you will be banished if you don't behave."

Cat ignored him and began to wash his face with delicate swipes of his paw.

Logan watched the cat for a moment as he pondered his next move. He wasn't about to retrieve the soggy towel with bare feet, so it looked like a naked dash to the bedroom was his only option. He heard an evil chuckle.

Writing appeared in the mist on the mirror. Leave, killer's spawn. A breathy whisper danced through his mind, chilling him all the way down the spine. "Killer's spawn."

He looked at the cat. Cat looked back at him, its golden eyes almost filled with large black pupils. It licked its lips and yawned.

As Logan stood on the cold, tiled floor, stark naked and dripping wet, he suddenly felt vulnerable. The cat stared at him. Suddenly afraid the cat would attack him, he made a dash for the bedroom. As he reached the door, it slammed shut, almost smashing into his face. He grabbed the handle and after a struggle, he managed to open it.

Anger exploded. Anger at the cat for making a mess in the bathroom, anger at the drafts slamming doors, and anger at himself for being rattled by what was happening. *Pull yourself together man. You'll be a cot case before the end of the week if you don't get your shit together.* His internal scolding didn't soothe him, but regardless nothing was going to make him believe ghosts existed. Whatever was happening had a human hand behind it, of that he was sure. It could only be Paige.

He slipped on some jeans, a T-shirt, and loafers. The rat-a-tat-tat at the front door jangled his already sizzling nerves. But immediately, he realized it was the pizza delivery. After collecting his pizza and doing a quick inspection of the house to ensure he was the only human occupant, he stoked the fire in the dining room hearth and settled down to eat.

He suspected the ruckus in the bathroom had been caused by Cat or some other animal trying to escape after coming through the open windows last night, but then... he couldn't explain the open windows. His thoughts went round and round in circles. Would Paige go to such lengths to get him out of the house? He didn't think so. It was an effort, but he pushed his ugly thoughts aside and grabbed up his sketch pad.

As he munched, he worked on ideas for the garden. He hadn't discussed the garden at all with Paige, so he couldn't begin anything. But it was relaxing to be creative. By the time he had finished his drawings and cleaned up the bathroom, it was nearly midnight. He carefully put the fire right out, just a little jumpy about leaving even smoldering embers in the hearth unattended, and crawled into his unmade bed. He gave a brief thought to his sexy dream the night before, smiled to himself, rolled over to his side, and closed his eyes.

***

His body hummed with pleasure. Hands slid over his buttocks, parting them, and sliding down the valley between them, pausing to slightly indent his butt hole before moving on to caress his balls. The fingers entangled themselves in the curly pubic hairs, pulling on them lightly. The hand encompassed his scrotum and squeezed gently before it moved to play with each of his balls, rolling them around inside their bag. His cock was already semi hard.

He groaned, and stirred restlessly. The sensations didn't stop. Strong hands urged him to turn over onto his back. She was there, naked. Her breasts right in his face. He reached up and cupped the nearest one and brought it to his mouth suckling strongly on the prominent nipple while his other hand slid over the soft curve of her abdomen and down to her thighs. This time, she made no attempt to stop him when he brought his hand back up and brushed it over the bushy red curls that hid her outer lips. He pressed his hand over her mound and rubbed firmly, bringing the outer lips tighter over her inner recesses. She moaned.

Emboldened, he slid his hand over the outer lips and towards her butt hole. He found it. It was tight and hot. He caressed it lightly then trailed his fingers down and slipped between her outer lips. He felt the moisture on them and dipped his fingers deeper in the liquid fire of her fluids until he found the opening to her pussy. He ran his finger around the opening. She squirmed, sighed then slowly reclined on to the pillow her legs slightly apart. He looked at her and pulled in a deep breath, almost overwhelmed by her delicate, white porcelain beauty. The symmetrical features, the English complexion, and the long, silken hair fanned out on the whiteness of the pillow were an intoxicating sight. His cock responded by hardening into a long throbbing rod. He leaned in, and one after the other, he suckled at her breasts. They were full and plump, the areola dark pools in which the rose pink nipples floated.

He cupped the fullness and massaged softly. Then he trailed down over her abdomen, as she had done to him the night before, but even as he did, he slid his hand over her mound and between her lips. Now he sought her pussy. He knew it was wet and warm. With careful exploration of each fold of moist pink flesh on the way, he found and teased her clit with the lightest of brushes with his fingers then moved on until he found her entrance. She was dripping. She adjusted her hips and opened her legs wider to give him easier access.

He pushed his finger just the tiniest bit into her then stopped. She moaned and lifted her hips to signal she wanted more. His cock throbbed and danced. It wanted more too. In response to her signals, he slid first one finger in the hot, encompassing passage and moved it around then he withdrew it before sliding two fingers in. Her pussy relaxed and softened at his insertion, so he thrust them in and out.

She sighed and moved her hips ever so slightly up and down. He slipped his fingers out and brought his hand to his face and took a deep breath. The wave of fiery need washed over him, almost sparking a premature ejaculation. He dropped his hand and this time inserted three fingers into her and wriggled them. He felt her muscles grip his fingers, release them, only to grip again. He looked at her face. Her eyes were open. She watched him from icy blue depths.

A sliver of unease rippled across his skin. He moved his fingers again, stroking the taut but flexible flesh of her vagina then searched until he found the small wrinkly spot. Almost immediately, he began to lightly tickle her G-spot, making her moan and writhe against his hand, her hips thrusting up against the pressure. As her breathing became more erratic, her breasts heaved with her struggle for enough air. He positioned himself between her parted legs and as he slipped his fingers out, he thrust his rock hard cock into her throbbing pussy.

Her hips rose to meet his downward thrust and he found his rod buried all the way to his balls into the wet, slippery inferno of her pussy. It was almost too hot, as the flesh grabbed and held him in a fierce grip. He thrust hard and fast, so aroused he could think of nothing other than the frenzied drive for his release. He heard her cry out, and her body pulsed against his throbbing flesh, her nails raking across his back. It was almost too much—exhilarating and frantic. He drove his organ deep and felt it erupt into a throbbing mass of pleasure, as he ejaculated hot cum against her cervix. His orgasm had barely concluded and his strength seeped away from him. An overwhelming weakness collapsed his arms and legs, even as he gasped in air and felt the sweat drip from his face.

***

He flopped over and found himself lying face down on the cool sheets, his face buried in the pillow. He was alone. His body spent, his cock tender, and his balls loose. He was sticky with cum and sexually satiated, but somehow it didn't quite have the soft glow he'd come to expect after a climax of such magnitude. He pulled himself out of bed and stumbled out the door. In a shaft of moonlight he saw Cat stalk up the passage. He followed the animal, but it vanished in the darkness. Sagging he fumbled his way to the bathroom and cleaned up. His head throbbed so he downed a couple of painkillers and staggered back to bed. He didn't bother to check the house. He knew he had only been dreaming.

He stirred kicking the tangled sheets from his legs. He could barely move. He dragged his eyes open and stared around the room. His thoughts knotted in his brain, his legs ached as if he'd climbed mountains in his sleep, and he had a raging headache—almost as if he was coming down with the flu. He struggled into consciousness and looked at his phone. It was one pm.

He slumped back on the bed and closed his eyes. He reached down to scratch his balls and hesitated. His cock felt tender, the sensitive skin seemed slightly roughened to the touch. He frowned as he remembered his dream. Damn it. Dream sex does not cause damage. He rolled over and buried his face in the pillow. A series of loud thumps on the front door reverberated through his head. He groaned.

He rolled over and sat on the edge of the bed. He held his head in his hands as it throbbed in response.

"Ok, I hear you. Hang on a moment." He pushed himself upright and dragged on jeans and a T-shirt.

"Ouch." The cloth raised a path of stinging pain down his back. He turned to the mirror and lifted the tee up. Warmth drained from his face, already a haggard grey. He had ten stripes of blood-encrusted gouges down the length of his back. "Oh shit." *What the fuck happened?* He moved carefully as they pulled and stung. He covered them with the T-shirt and went to the door.

Two men stood on the front verandah, an older man and a young guy who seemed hardly old enough to be an apprentice. "You Logan Dunsford-Hamilton?"

Logan nodded and held out his hand. "You must be Davey Cawthen and son—the stonemason."

The older man smiled. "I am indeed. Now, we'll inspect the areas needing repairs first, don't need your help for that mate, and let you go back to bed."

"What?"

"Well, if you don't mind me saying so, mate, you look like death warmed up."

"Yes, I feel like it too. Think I might be getting the flu or something."

"I'll push the quote under the door. You can let me know about the new stone work later."

Logan nodded.

While the two men inspected the foundations and stone walls, Logan dragged himself into the shower. As he slipped under the stream of water, he heard a whisper.

"This is only the beginning, killer's spawn—leave my house or die."

The plastic curtain billowed out before it slapped back against him. It clung tightly, holding him under the stream of steaming water. He gasped for breath. He fought the plastic, tearing it from the rings on the rail. It dropped to the wet tiles and lay still. He turned the water off and climbed out. His back was a raging mass of stinging pain and as he dried himself, he found blood on his towel. A lump of unease settled in his gut. There was no way those scratches were caused by him or an irritation. Even so, his mind shied away from the turbulence of his vivid sexual dream, and the feel of his ghostly lover's nails raking down his back. He refused to entertain the thought there might be more to his sexual exploits than adult wet dreams caused by too much celibacy.

He took his coffee, toast and headache tablets outside and perched on a rickety seat by the old wooden table on the lawn and soaked up some of the mild sunshine. His head seemed clearer now, but his back still hurt, and the soft material of his boxer briefs seemed like sandpaper against his cock and balls.

Paige was due to move in tomorrow. He was more than ready to end his solitary time. Perhaps having a real woman in the house—and a very attractive one, at that—would ease his dreams. He was worried about getting too close to his new housemate. He couldn't deny his attraction but deep down, slivers of mistrust dug away at him. She claimed not to remember those childhood incidents, but he did. Besides, he didn't want to get embroiled in another relationship. Not right now—maybe not ever.

There would be enough negotiation needed with the joint money for the renovations to cause angst without getting intimately involved. He didn't trust her and she didn't have any respect for him. End of story.

The stonemason appeared with the repair quote.

"Feeling better mate?"

"Yeah. I'll live. Might as well do the lot while you're here. "

After extensive discussions with the stonemason, Logan thought the quote for the repair of the existing stone and the building of the extension was reasonable, so he signed off right there and then. They promised to start on the repairs in a couple of days, so they would be ready to begin the extension as soon as the footings were ready. The tree lopper came, and they discussed how the removal of the Norfolk

Island pine would be managed. The rest of the afternoon, Logan made phone calls.

By the time it was getting dark, Logan had a throbbing headache and felt so lethargic, he merely ordered pizza to be delivered again and sat by the fire to eat it.

He couldn't eliminate the growing apprehension he felt about the night, so he opened a bottle of good red wine and drank his way to the bottom. Feeling mellow under the influence of the wine, he stretched out in the deep recliner and stared into space. He struggled with his thoughts—and his uneasiness. He'd always been scathing about the paranormal, but these past couple of nights had shaken that strong opinion to the core. Unable to resolve his internal conflict, he shut his eyes and tried to blank his brain.

He jerked awake. A door thudded shut a second time, followed by a screech, and the sound of shattering glass. Logan leaped out of the chair and charged through the house, turning on all the lights as he went. In the lounge room, he found the ornate gilded mirror smashed into a thousand pieces and in the temporary kitchen, the fridge was open. Food and crockery were spread all over the room.

Logan's temper exploded.

"Quit it, you damn bitch—ghost, spirit, demon or whatever you are. Enough already. This is my house. Get out. Stay out. And stay out of my bed, while you're at it," he bellowed. He gasped air in. Before he could duck, a can of soup and a tub of butter hurtled towards him. The butter caught him right in the eye then dropped to the floor and splattered. The can of soup flew past and hit the wall.

"Damn you. Go to hell," he yelled, as he wiped the butter off his face.

"I'm already in hell, killer's spawn. It's time you joined me. Leave or die."

Logan spun around then back again, sure the voice was from right beside him. He twitched then swallowed deeply before shaking his head. The room was empty. *Oh boy I've got it bad. I'm talking to it now. God help me.* His knees softened. He grabbed the edge of the table as he surveyed the damage. Bloody hell. He heard the swish. He looked up. The light glinted on the blade the knife hovered in the air. *Holy shit.* He lunged for the doorway, fell through the gap and hauled the door shut behind him. The knife thudded into the wood. More thuds followed. He wanted to leave the house, but an innate stubbornness bore down on him. "I won't leave. Do you hear me I won't leave."

He scrambled to his feet and lurched down the passage. He locked the lounge door behind him and slumped into his chair. He stoked up the fire. It was going to be a long night. His head lolled. He jerked awake; surveyed the room, added more wood to the fire then snatched up his sketch pad. The intoxicating lethargy of sleep slipped over him. He forced his eyes open and gripped the pencil he held. He saw the squiggles on the page. He was losing the battle to stay awake. Sleep beckoned. He resisted. A warm sweet lassitude blanketed him. He snuggled into it and closed his eyes—just for a moment...

***

She was there, kneeling beside him. His fly was already unzipped, and his trunks pulled down far enough to expose his cock. Her mouth was sliding up and down his shaft. Her head moved in a quick, urgent rhythm. Her fingers caressed in between his balls and his butt hole. He trembled as his simmering sexual appetite flared under her expert licking and sucking. He watched her caress him, and was powerless to stop her. He reached out to halt her motion, but she shook his hand from her head and continued to slide her mouth up and down his shaft. He made no attempt to touch her in return, but just lay there and sank into the exquisite throbbing of his cock as it built towards a climax. He couldn't stop himself thrusting as the urge to explode washed over him. Then it was there. He groaned and thrust upwards and hot cum squirted into her mouth. She made no attempt to pull away, only pausing a second to swallow his fluids then she continued to suck until he was dry. He flopped back in the chair. He watched as she drew away. She wasn't smiling. He reached out to her, but his hands found nothing.

The clatter of embers falling from the grate pulled him back to the room. His limbs weighed heavy. Uncoordinated movements barely managed to replace them in the hearth. As he stood, his legs almost buckled under him, and he sank back into the chair. He lay motionless, unable to motivate himself to move. Despite his fatigue, he didn't sleep until the sun was up and the magpies were singing on the lawn outside. The fire was out. He pulled himself out of the chair and staggered like a drunk to his room. He fell with a thump onto his bed. He didn't undress or even pull the blankets up before he sank into oblivion.

Chapter Three

Paige had brought groceries as promised and headed straight for the kitchen. The house was silent and deserted, and she wondered if Logan was out on an errand. As she entered the kitchen, she stumbled to a halt. The room was a disaster site. Food was scattered around the room—on the floor, up the walls and in the sink. The fridge hung open, pumping cold air into the room. Crockery, including her favorite dinner set, lay smashed into jagged shards that punctuated the food. A knife was embedded in the back of the door. *My God what the hell happened?*

She heard a noise. The ginger cat sat in the middle of the table, delicately washing its paws and wiping its face. It meowed at her, stood up, and swished its tail. "So kitty did you do this?" Automatically, she reached out to pat it before she remembered what it had done to Logan. She withdrew her hand.

The cat looked longingly at her and meowed again. Paige felt silly then. Maybe this cat just didn't like men. She reached out and scratched it under the chin. It purred and rubbed its head over her hand. The cat looked at her with golden eyes that seemed to know more than a cat should. It mewled softly at her, then with a sharp flick of its tail, jumped off the table and stalked out the door.

Leaving the mess in the kitchen, Paige went in search of Logan. She didn't get worried about him until she came across the smashed mirror in the lounge room. *What the hell had gone on here? Had there been burglars? Had Logan done this?*

She hurried down the passage, grabbing a fire poker on the way to his room. She knocked loudly on the door and heard him groan from inside.

"Logan, are you all right? Do you need help?"

She heard shuffling, and the door opened. She gasped at the apparition before her. He was unshaven, pale, bleary-eyed and hunched over, as though in pain.

"Good grief, Logan, you look like hell."

He tried to smile, but it was just a faded replica of the brilliant smile she'd been subjected to in the lawyer's office.

Logan leaned on the door frame for support. "I feel like hell. Haven't been sleeping very well the last few nights."

She tipped her head to one side and looked him up and down. She would have blamed something far more potent than a few sleepless nights. Booze or drugs? Illness? For goodness sake, what had she gotten herself into this time?

Logan spied her weapon, and he scowled. "What's that for?"

Paige waved the poker in the air. "To defend myself, if required. After I saw the kitchen and the lounge room, I thought it might be wise to be prepared."

He gave a small grumble of laughter. "The way I feel right now, all you would need is a decent puff of air to knock me flat. Give me half an hour for a shower, and I'll make you a coffee."

"You do realize there's a huge mess in the kitchen."

He leaned on the door, a frown puckered his face. "Oh damn, I forgot."

Even though she was having serious second thoughts about her new housemate, she went ahead and brought her suitcases in. By the time she had unloaded her car and stowed her personal luggage in her room, Logan was dressed and looking slightly better than before. She was beginning to wonder what Logan was going to be like to live with. Her arrival had not been the auspicious start she had expected.

"So, do you want to explain this then?" She pointed at the mess.

Logan shrugged. "Nothing to explain, really. I accidently left some windows open last night. I think it was a couple of possums. Anyway, I was too tired to clean it up before."

She looked around the room in disgust. "Possums? Really, Logan? You think possums did this." She pointed at the knife. "And this?"

He frowned down at her now. He obviously didn't like being questioned. "Yes, I do, Paige... or maybe the damn cat, but I'm sure as hell it wasn't your beloved ghost."

Up clunked her defensive wall. "She is not my 'beloved' ghost, but you needn't scoff, for there is a ghost. You could at least show me respect by admitting the truth."

They faced each other over the mess. Logan still glared at her, but she saw the flush creeping up his face. She glared back at him, daring him, willing him, to speak the truth.

"Look, Paige. I can't explain this or the other things that have been happening. Can we just leave it be for the moment?"

She nodded, knowing he would most likely tell the truth if she didn't pressure him.

***

Together they cleaned the kitchen and put away the groceries. He showed her the room he'd started on, especially the beautiful timber floors that had been hidden by the shabby, old-fashioned carpet. Back in the dining room, now the kitchen, she perched on one of the two stools on offer.

"Are these the revised plans you have drawn up for the restoration of the house?"

Logan nodded. "Have a look over the drawings and the list while we have coffee. The garden one is underneath. They're just ideas, of course." Logan made coffee. He knew she hadn't bought his explanation about possums. He'd surprised himself when it had come unbidden out of his mouth. But he wasn't ready to share the experiences he couldn't explain.

He carried the coffee to the table and sat opposite her. While he watched her study the plans, he tried to think through the stuff that had happened. He knew she would razz him about the ghost and he was not sure he was ready to admit it yet. If he admitted to her that the ghost existed, he had to accept certain other claims she'd made in the past might have a sliver of truth and he wasn't sure he could do that, just yet.

She chewed her bottom lip as she concentrated on the intricate line drawings and made her own notes.

He watched her. Her eyes were soft violet-blue underneath a long fringe of strawberry blonde hair that was cut into a short, shaggy bob. Tiny blue-green pearl studs decorated her ears. Her thin cotton shirt was a reasonably firm fit, and it clung to the soft curves of her bust. His breath became uneven. She was perfect all round. He breathed deeply, her scent intoxicating.

"So what do you think?"

She smiled up at him. "It's a big job, but nothing we can't handle. I see you have already organized the stonemasons and the tree's removal."

"I thought it was best to get going on the structural things first, I mean, with winter coming soon." He sipped his coffee and watched her.

Paige looked up at him and smiled. "I have no objections. We had already decided they needed to be done."

A rush of wind swept over them—papers, plans and color samples swirled into the air, spun around, and slapped at Logan. He backed up and out of the door, trying to escape the sting of the flying debris. As he backed through the door, it slammed hard and loud in his face.

He heard Paige scream then scramble to open the door. It refused to budge.

"Logan, let me out. What damn game are you playing?"

"I'm not playing games, Paige. It's the house," Logan yelled back.

"The house! You mean the ghost?"

"Damn it, Paige. Ghosts do not exist."

"Well explain this then."

With a savage swipe, the door swung open. Logan stumbled through the opening as if pushed. He fell to his knees in front of Paige. She stumbled back and fell to the floor. Logan staggered to his feet and rushed toward her. She stared up at him as she shuffled backwards.

"Paige, it wasn't me." He held out his hand.

"Is this one of the things you can't explain? You're not going to blame me for this."

Her eyes were wide. Uncertainty darkened the color. Shit, she's really scared of being accused. She seems to have really taken my accusations to heart. Perhaps I should've been kinder—we were kids after all. "I'm not going to blame you, for this or the other 'incidents'. Come on up you get."

***

Finally, she took his hand and allowed him to pull her to her feet.

Logan shrugged, and held his hands wide in a gesture of surrender. "You win, okay. I can't explain any of the things that have happened here in the last week, other than to accept your assertion the house is haunted by a ghost and whoever it—she—is, she really does not want me here."

"She has never been violent..." She stopped, knowing even as she spoke, it wasn't true. A dusty, but painful memory slipped out past the door she'd kept shut all these years. "Oh my God, yes she has. I remember now—that time in the big shed when the rack of tools toppled over on you. That must have been her. The adults blamed me. They said I was climbing on it, but I wasn't. It just fell. I really don't think she likes you."

"Yes, but why? It seems she didn't want me in the house all those years ago either. In fact, I thought you were trying to kill me. Sarah and your mother were the only ones who believed in your ghost; everyone else thought it was you... even your father."

Her father didn't believe her. A sudden stab of pain cut through her mind. Her father. There was something she needed to remember about her father. About that time in the house.

The color drained from her face and a hardness shone in her eyes. She was thinking, deeply. Something he said had worried her. "I sort of saw her the other night—long full skirts, ringlets, and a bonnet. It wasn't all that clear," he said. "But her message was. She told me to get out or die."

She looked directly at him now, a deep frown marring her face. "If she doesn't want you here, Logan, you could be in danger."

"Hey, anyone here?"

Relief rushed through him at the distraction. "Looks like the guys for the kitchen extension are here."

***

As Paige followed the men around, she was glad they'd made all the hard decisions about the house, including architectural drawings, quotes and council approvals, in the days before they had actually moved in. Things would hopefully go smoothly in view of all their preplanning.

Despite the resentment she felt towards Logan for his childhood indiscretions, she couldn't help but admire his gorgeous body. At six foot three, he was perfectly proportioned with broad shoulders, hard, defined pecs and shapely biceps that told of hours in the gym to enhance his naturally chiseled shape. There wasn't a spare ounce of flesh on him. His low-slung jeans clung to slim hips and draped over a shapely backside before encasing long, solid legs. His smoky grey-blue eyes were decidedly cute, especially when half filled with sleep.

She forced her mind back to the discussion going on around her. The plan was to completely demolish the old kitchen and extend it to twice the size, with the outer walls made up of a lot of glass to catch the morning sun. The new area would be built in the style of the rest of the house. It would be costly, but both of them had agreed it would be worth it.

With the final assessment of the site completed and paperwork checked the contractors promised to begin tomorrow as previous arranged.

***

It was cozy, almost domestic as they prepared dinner together later that evening. Logan grilled the steaks while she prepared a salad. She watched him out of the corner of her vision, he was confident in the kitchen. He looked better tonight than he had when she'd arrived. There was some life back in his eyes and color in his face. She had to admit she was a little nervous about her first night in the house. She wasn't sure what to expect—if anything—from him or the ghostly inhabitant.

He placed her steak in front of her and slipped into his seat. "No second thoughts about fulfilling the requirements of this inheritance. You have been very quiet since the incident in here this afternoon. I can assure you, you have nothing to fear living in the house with me."

"I know. I don't have anything to fear from you, but I suspect you have something to fear from the ghost. She doesn't want you here. She has never wanted you in this house. I don't know why, but I will not take the blame if you get hurt, or worse, like I did when I was a kid."

She reached for the salad and her hand collided with his. He took her hand in a firm grasp, then encompassed it with both hands.

"I'm not going to blame you for anything."

"But you did, Logan, all those years ago. You blamed me for the shelving. You told your parents I pushed it over. I was only three-and-a-half. There is no way I could have even shaken that shelf, let alone pushed it over. To this day I believe the ghost did it, but I took the blame."

"So you do remember?"

She shook her head. "I began to remember little bits after our first visit to the house, but there is more I must remember. Something very bad happened. I can't explain it, but thinking about it fills me with dread and pain—and terrible guilt."Today she had been afraid.

Her elusive memories stirred. The sound of his scream as the shelf fell on him echoed in her head. A cold sweat popped out on her skin. Had she pushed it—really pushed it over—on purpose? She didn't know—she couldn't remember—and that's what scared her.

"You were only a baby," Logan said. "Why should you feel guilt? I mean, even if you did do anything on purpose, you wouldn't have known the consequences." Logan shrugged. "There were several incidents—a run-away car and the day I nearly drowned in the dam."

His words hit her like punches thrown in a drunken brawl. Pain like physical blows. She cringed. "But surely..." She shook her head. "I don't remember."

"Don't fret about it. All I really remember clearly was your dad. He was absolutely livid at you and furious at your mum because she wouldn't take it seriously. Your mum and dad argued violently."

Paige held her head. It throbbed so bad she thought it was going to explode. "It was your fault, Logan, that they argued," she burst out. "You blamed me for everything, Dad blamed me. Damn it, I can't remember everything that happened."

His large hands were warm, the skin slightly roughened. His thumb gently caressed her palm.

His touch sent sparks of awareness along her skin. It had been a while since she had been interested in any man. It was dangerous to become involved with Logan, but she didn't know why.

He lifted her hand, kissed her palm then kissed each of her finger tips in turn. Each caress was firm, but brief. As he kissed her hand, he watched her from shadowed grey-blue eyes. She saw the question in his eyes—a plea for her trust.

"I made them blame you. I blamed you. I thought it was you—now I am not so sure, but we both need to let it go because it was all a long time ago."

"Maybe, but what happened had terrible consequences, if only I could remember. You need to be careful, Logan. I believe being in this house is not good for you. Being with me, in this house, is not good for you."

He smiled. "It's all good. Go on. Eat your steak. It's getting cold."

She smiled, even as she pulled her hand away and reached for the salad. The thing she feared the most was herself. "There is a lock on your bedroom door, you know, if you feel unsafe. I saw it this morning."

He stared at her for a moment, a look of comical surprise transformed his expression. Seconds later his laughter rolled out of his chest in a warm, husky rumble. He dropped his gaze and picked up his cutlery, even as his body vibrated with amusement.

Her attraction to him flared in a burst of fiery sexual awareness. She could bed this man very easily, except for what he had instigated all those years ago.

***

When they parted for the night, he paused before closing his door. He smiled. He felt better knowing she was not afraid of him, but wondered at her concern for him. She claimed not to remember, but he wasn't quite sure he believed her. Something about her memories had obviously distressed her.

***

He'd barely closed eyes when she appeared by his bed, her feminine curves naked, and lit only by the silvery light of the moon. He looked into her face, framed by the mane of strawberry hair. He started. Except for the hair, he would have sworn it was Paige. An urgent ache in his groin prodded him, and he moved over to allow her access to his bed.

She laid beside him, on her back, her voluptuous breasts settling onto her chest.

He reached out and laid his hand over one. It was firm and plump, but soft at the same time. He reached down and took the nipple in his mouth. The nub was hard and erect and he circled his tongue around its base, tasting her scent before he took it in his mouth and suckled, first gently then harder, pulling the taut protrusion out from the surrounding, soft flesh. With his thumb and finger he teased the other nipple pulling it out then stroking the top.

She moaned in pleasure, but pushed him down as she parted her legs.

He moved down, kissing her flesh as he went, until he settled himself between her legs. With both hands he opened the outer folds to reveal the darker pinks of the moist inner lips, and the even darker flesh that was the entrance to her pussy. He stroked his finger up and down the lips, using her juices as lubricant. Then he dipped his fingers into her entrance and spread her heated moisture upwards to the nub of her clit. It was already erect, protruding from the surrounding softness.

He took it between finger and thumb and slid with a tiny up and down motion along its length as he inserted two fingers into her pussy. He turned them this way and that in time with his strokes of her clit.

She moaned. She writhed and pushed her hips up against his fingers.

He increased the speed at which he was moving his fingers and pushed deeper. Then he felt it, the clenching and trembling of her muscles as she arched her back and cried out.

He felt the gush of fluid against his hand as it squirted out of her pussy. He moved up and licked her clit then sucked on it tenderly.

Moments later, she stiffened and shuddered with another orgasm. She cried out, a screeching howl.

He didn't stop his stroking and licking, even when he felt her sag and soften in the aftershocks of her climax. His cock throbbed, his balls ached to be touched, but he was patient until he felt her tighten with a new round of tension. Then he lifted himself over her, took his hands away and eased his stiffened penis deep into her. It slid in so easily, the silken flesh and juices hot on his swollen sensitive skin. He thrust hard and deep.

She whimpered.

He kept thrusting. The feel of her enveloping his flesh was mind blowing. He thrust deep. He felt her cervix collide with his head then withdrew and sank again into the hot glove of her dripping flesh. This time his balls almost went in too and he rubbed them tight up against her butt. An exquisite pleasure that was almost pain shot through him. He held back his need to explode and thrust again and again.

She moaned.

He felt her pussy tighten and begin to undulate along its length, grabbing and releasing his throbbing cock. He felt her shudder and he thrust fast and deep. Then he let go and exploded, spilling hot cum the full length of her vagina as his climax rolled through him in a thunderous wave. He buried himself deep in her, arched his back and stilled as the sensations pulsed along his cock. He was drained. He felt exhausted, even as his cock softened and slipped out. He laid his body on hers, his head resting on her breasts.

He moaned his total satiation and wrapped his arms around her. He woke to find himself alone, in the bed, clutching his pillow to his chest, his body and sheets sticky with sexual fluids. He could barely push himself upright. He looked around the room. It was empty. He looked at his phone; it showed four am. He slumped back on the bed, and stared into space, his body aching with sexual release and tiredness.

***

She jerked awake. Her body trembled with the sudden transition. Burning needles of tension prickled in her gut. What woke me? It was very dark. She lay motionless, listening, watching the dark. Then she heard it. Moans and cries coming from Logan's room. Sexual moans and cries. The rustle of sheets and creak of the bed. The motions of their bodies and the accompanying grunts.

Bloody hell. He could have warned me he was having company, and they could damn well have the decency to keep it quiet.

She tried not to listen. It was impossible not to hear. Irritated she rolled onto her side. She pulled a pillow over her head. Ever so slightly muted the sexual sounds seemed even more intoxicating. An indiscriminate ache between her legs, then a tightening of her nipples, and warmth seeped through her body. She tossed and turned, trying to ignore her awareness.

***

Soft rain fell. The bed was warm and a languid sense of contentment wrapped around her as she stretched. Then she remembered. Maybe, she would get to meet Logan's noisy lover over breakfast. She raced through the shower, dressed in some old clothes, and adjourned to the kitchen to heat the kettle, not wanting to be caught unprepared for the unknown woman who shared Logan's bed.

Moments later, she heard a truck rumble up the drive. She looked at the time. Seven. Looks like an early start for the demolition guys here to do the kitchen. The kettle had barely boiled when there was a thump on the back door. There was no sign of Logan, and that irritated her. If he could stay up all night having hot sex with his lover then he could damn well get up, and show these blokes what to do.

A tall muscular man of obvious Mediterranean descent grinned at her when she opened the door. She recognized him immediately as the demolition contractor they had hired earlier. He had a stainless steel machine under one arm and a bag of roasted coffee beans hanging from the other hand. "I can put this in the kitchen to make coffee?"

"Of course you can, Antonio. "

"You call me Tony, most people do."

She smiled. "So Tony, you don't like the instant kind?"

"Mamma mia! That is no better than dishwater, Bella. I'll show you what is real coffee later, but first we need to put up all the protective sheeting so you don't get too much dust inside when we knock the walls down." Once his coffee machine was safely installed, Tony marched outside, and began giving orders, loudly, in a mix of Italian and English.

Paige retreated to the quiet of the temporary kitchen, and reheated the kettle. While it boiled, she marched down the passage and knocked impatiently on Logan's door. "Hey, lover boy, wakey, wakey. Rise and shine. Tony's here."

Silence from within.

She knocked again. "Logan. Damn it, wake up."

A groan rumbled under the door before it trailed off into silence.

She rapped on the door again. "If you don't respond, I'm going to come right in, regardless of your company, or your state of undress."

Silence.

"Damn it, Logan, I'm coming in." She turned the handle, and pushed the door open.

He lay on the top of the sheet, totally naked. The covers lay on the floor in a jumbled pile. He was alone in the bed. Obviously his company hadn't stayed the night. His face was pasty grey under the dark shadow of beard growth; his eyes were closed. His broad, muscular chest moved up and down, ever so slightly. His abdomen was a beautifully sculpted six-pack that slid into narrow hips, long muscular legs, and big feet. His chest was almost hairless, but a narrow trail of dark, springy hair led from his navel to his cock. Right now, his cock lay soft and relaxed, curving down over his balls with their sprinkling of dark pubic hair. He was well endowed, thick and long, even flaccid as he was.

Her pussy tingled as she perved and appreciated. Her hands itched to touch, to stroke, and to caress. Snatching control of her desires Paige stalked across the room. She flicked the sheet over him, then grabbed his shoulder and shook him. "Wake up, Logan. Tony's here."

He groaned, and turned away from her nudging.

"Oh, my God, Logan! What happened to your back?" Her screeched question failed to elicit a response. Paige stared at the sight of the long, blood encrusted scratches that scarred his back. She grabbed his shoulder again. "Wake up!"

This time he dragged his eyes half open. "Paige?"

"Yes, Logan, it's Paige."

His lids drooped. She snatched up the bottle of water from the bedside table, wrenched the lid off, and poured the contents on his face.

He spluttered, coughed, and sat upright, wiping the cold water away. A savage glare twisting his face. "What the hell did you do that for?"

"I did it because you would not wake up."

"I feel like shit. So tired... every muscle aches like I've been bashed up."

She put her hands on her hips and scowled down at him. "Well, that's what happens when one spends all night romping around the bedroom having energetic, noisy sex with a screaming banshee of a lover. You get no sympathy from me. You two kept me awake half the night."

"But I didn't... "

She cut of his feeble protest. "Don't lie, Logan. I don't care if you have a lover over, but I would appreciate it if you warned me, and if the two of you kept it down to a dull roar, so I could sleep. A little respect, okay?"

"Paige, I swear I did not have a woman in my bed. I did dream about having sex with the same beautiful woman, like all the other nights since I have been here at the house..."

"Don't give me that. I heard you... and her. She moaned and screamed her pleasure at the top of her lungs" Paige slapped her hands on her hips her words sharp and snappy. She hated that he was lying to her.

He shook his head. "I was alone."

She ignored the assertion he was alone. "And another thing, what did you do to your back. It's ripped open and covered in blood. Some of the scratches look infected."

He looked up at her now, his expression grim, his eyes dull, and his mouth drawn into a thin line. "I have no idea what happened to my back. I woke up with the scratches yesterday."

"Well, when you finish in the shower, I am going to bathe them in antiseptic. No arguments."

He nodded. "Just give me a moment, and I'll be right out to guide Tony."

***

Half an hour later he came into the kitchen, clad in a pair of faded jeans that clung deliciously snug to his hips and crotch.

Knowing what was hidden behind the zippered fly was almost more intoxicating to her than actually seeing him naked.

He held his T-shirt in his hands. "You said you would have a look at my back." He moved closer hesitantly.

She nodded.

Logan sat on the stool, and turned it slightly, so she could see his back. "It bled on the towel again." He sounded hounded and contrite.

Paige opened the first-aid kit and pulled out some of what she needed. His back was indeed bleeding from a couple of spots, while others looked red and inflamed. She bathed each scratch in antiseptic and hot water.

He sat silently in front of her, his head hung down, as he stared at the floor.

She guessed he wasn't seeing the floor, and that something troubled him. A couple of times he flinched at her ministrations.

She had nearly finished before he spoke.

"I slept alone last night. I... I keep having these vivid dreams though—so vivid they could be real. A beautiful woman comes to me each night—so beautiful. It's like she bewitches me. The sex is mind blowing. I can't seem to resist. Then I wake up, and I'm alone. I know it was only a dream even though... even though all the physical signs are there that I had sex with a real woman—even these scratches."

"Dream lovers do not inflict wounds like this, Logan." Paige finished off bathing the wounds.

"I know. I don't know how to explain it." His voice trailed off into silence.

"Then don't." She sounded snappish, but she would rather not know than have him lie about it. She finished the last dressing. "Ok, that should do you for now. You better go check on Tony."

Annoyance surged through her. *Damn it, she had heard them. Why was he lying? Did all men feel the need to lie, even when there was no trade off in doing so?* She shook her head to banish her ugly thoughts. *Surely not? Well, she didn't want to believe it of Logan, but past history assured her he was a very good liar and that bothered her. Was she already in trouble, as far as her emotions were concerned?*

***

Paige wandered outside.

Logan waved her over.

Paige looked over the worksite. "How's the demolition going, fellas?"

"The roof is completed and we should have the first wall mostly demolished by knock off time, but we'll definitely get the chimney safe before we leave today." Tony perched himself on an empty crate.

"We have made progress. Grab a seat, Paige. The apprentice has gone to get KFC for lunch. This is Tony Franco, his son, Joseph, and the apprentice—when he gets back—is Adamo. So, how did it go with your unpacking?"

"All done."

"Good."

Paige smiled. "It's going to be gorgeous when it is all finished. I can just imagine the sun streaming in the windows on a cool winter morning."

Adamo appeared with a couple of buckets of KFC and it was all quiet for a while.

***

With the food eaten the men set about constructing scaffolding around the chimney, now just a tower of loosely mortared bricks. It was exacting work that Tony supervised closely.

Paige stayed well back out of the way.

Logan stood in the center of the kitchen and watched Joe carefully scaffold the top of the chimney where the mortar had perished.

The young builder wobbled and grabbed for the scaffolding. "Below!" he yelled as half a dozen bricks hurtled down, directly at Logan.

Logan dived out of the way, but it was as if they were being thrown at him, because despite moving, two caught him glancing blows to the side of the head.

Chapter Four

Paige jumped to her feet as she heard the cry of warning. She'd seen the bricks fall. Logan was crumpled on the floor. She ran to him and shook him gently.

"Logan, Logan, can you hear me? It's Paige." No response. She removed the bricks from on top of his head. One of the wounds was pouring blood. The second hadn't seemed to have broken the skin, but she could feel the scalp swelling under her fingers.

"Tony, get the first-aid kit from the other room."

"No need, Bella. We have one for the site." Tony knelt by her side, a large first-aid kit in his hand. "Should I call an ambulance?"

"Yes. Is Joe okay?"

"He is shaking... stupido. I told him the bricks were unstable." Tony grumbled as he opened the kit and then shook his finger at his son.

"But, Papa, I was pushed out of the way. Someone pushed the bricks..."

Tony cuffed his son around the ears. "Stupido. Ah, the younger generation always knows best. Stupido."

Joe put a hand to his stinging ear and glared back at his father. "But, Papa..."

"Hey, you two, stop arguing and call that ambulance."

She placed a pad over the bleeding wound and applied pressure to stop the flow of blood. Then, with Tony's help, she carefully turned Logan on his side, and put him in the recovery position. "Go Adamo to the end bedroom and get the duvet." As soon as the young man brought it she tucked this around him as she monitored his pulse and breathing. He seemed to be breathing okay, but Paige was glad when she heard the ambulance screaming towards them.

An hour later, with Logan gone to hospital and the workers knocked off, Paige went inside to lock everything up and retrieved his car keys. She hadn't asked his permission, but he was parked behind her. As she went to leave his bedroom, she heard a sound—muted almost, coming from a distance. A soft, mournful sobbing. A tingle of unease raced over her skin. She felt the cat weaving around her ankles, rubbing itself up against her. It purred loudly. She looked around, but could not place the source of the crying.

Leaving the light burning in the hallway she walked quickly up the passage with the cat trotting behind her, its tail straight up in the air like a mast. It was gloomy inside, although the sun had barely reached the horizon, and her skin tingled with unease as the sound of sobbing followed her. She wanted to run, but she forced herself to walk sedately out the back door. The cat came out with her and sat serenely at her feet, as she locked the door behind her. A voice drifted over the garden, just a whisper, so faint it might as well have been the wind in the Norfolk Island pine that towered over the house.

"Go from here, Daughter. Go from this place. Go before the killer's spawn gets you."

Paige opened the car door but paused and listened. She strained to hear the words, but now all she could hear was the shush and whisper of the evening breeze in the pine branches.

She slid into the car and slammed the door shut. An echoing thud made her jump. The cat stood on the bonnet, glaring in through the windscreen at her. When she started the engine, the cat screeched and jumped to the ground. She backed out carefully, acutely aware she was driving a BMW that didn't belong to her.

The doctor was still stitching Logan's head when she arrived, and he'd decreed Logan would be kept overnight for observation. She was ushered into a small cubicle to see him when the doctor had finished. He looked pale under the large dressing on the left side of his head that extended down onto his forehead.

"How're you feeling?" she asked.

"Got a shocking headache, but then that's to be expected when one is hit with a brick or two. Is Joe okay?"

Paige pulled up a chair. "Joe's fine, but Tony is hopping mad with him. Says he was stupid."

Logan frowned as he tried to concentrate. "I would say it wasn't entirely his fault. It seemed a bit targeted for an accident."

"So, are you going to blame me for this too? Do you think I threw the bricks?" she hissed under her breath.

"No. Of course I'm not blaming you. You weren't up on the chimney. Please don't be so sensitive about things. I don't think Joe pushed those bricks either. I moved as they came down, but they still hit me. Maybe it was your ghost."

"Logan, from a man who scoffed at ghosts less than a fortnight ago, you're now really playing that card for all it's worth. Better keep quiet about it in here. After a bash on the head, they might lock you in a straitjacket. Headlines won't look so good either; 'Prominent Wealthy South Australian Businessman Believes Ghost is Trying to Kill Him'."

"You don't seem bothered by her when you're in the house. Why is she picking on me?" He sounded peeved and sulky.

Paige shrugged. "She's never bothered me, or anyone else that I know of. It's not men in general, because she never seemed to have a problem with my father when we stayed over. Really, I'm hardly aware of her—well... except for tonight."

"Well?"

Logan had been watching her more closely than she anticipated and seen her slight hesitation.

"Something's happened, hasn't it?"

"Well, not really, Logan. Just tonight, when I went to get your car keys... oh, by the way, I am driving your car. I hope that's okay?"

He dismissed her use of his car with a wave of his hand. "No problem, but what about tonight?" As he tried to push himself more upright on the pillows, his machines beeped faster.

Paige glanced at them. "You're upsetting yourself. Lie back."

He obeyed, but still watched her face intently, his grey-blue eyes deeply shadowed and a little unfocused.

"Tonight, I thought I heard sobbing in your bedroom. It seemed to follow me all the way through the house. The cat was also in the house—you know the ginger one that hangs around. Anyway, I suspect the noise was the wind or an animal. Funny though, for the first time ever, I found it a bit spooky in the old house alone."

"Could it be the ghost crying?"

Paige shook her head. "Maybe, but I don't think she's sorry she hurt you. More likely just the whisper of wind in that huge great pine. It did sound like a woman's voice though, but it was probably my heightened emotions working overtime."

Logan eased himself on the pillows. "What did the voice say?"

She immediately wished she hadn't mentioned it. It bothered her to see this intelligent and talented man brought to such anguish by something he thought he was imagining."

"Paige?"

"Look, I'm sure I imagined a voice that said 'Go from here. Go before the killer's spawn gets you.' Or something like that... just the wind in that pine."

Logan rested his head on the pillows. "Will you promise me something? Don't go into the house alone tonight, please?"

"Logan, I am not spooked by the house and—" She fell silent as his words cut her off.

"I know you're comfortable with ghosts and such, but I'm not, and I can't rest easy in here if you don't promise."

Paige sighed. "All right. If it makes you feel more comfortable, I won't go in the house until after I come back tomorrow and pick you up."

"You must listen to your man, beautiful lady. It be best if neither of you ever return to that house."

Paige looked around. A wizened up, very old lady, stood at the door of the cubicle. She had a gnarled, swarthy complexion and huge gold hoops in her ears. Her head was covered with a scarf threaded with gold.

"I beg your pardon?"

The old woman shuffled forward. "I warn you, beautiful lady. Your man is being hunted by a Qarinah—a spirit, a ghost. I see it in his aura. She is sucking his life force out of him. She intends to kill him."

"Come on, Grandma. Stop scaring the poor people with your stories. Sorry, guys. Grandma is very old; her mind wanders back to the old days."

The young man ushered the old woman away, but she turned and waggled her finger.

"The Qarinah will kill him—be warned, beautiful lady."

Logan and Paige looked at each other.

Paige couldn't form any words that would have made sense. The warning was just a little bit too close to their reality for comfort. A memory leapt into her mind. She started back from the vividness of it—the memory of a voice that whispered dangerous thoughts to her. She saw the ghost in her mind for a moment, urging her to do things, saying, 'He must die; he will never have my house. Help me child. Help me rid the world of this menace.' Paige gasped as the memory filled her mind—pulling the leaky boat into the dam, getting in, and urging Logan to join her. She tried to remember what happened, but the next sliver of memory was of her standing with Sarah on the muddy bank, watching her father drag a limp Logan from the water. She cringed inside. Did I do that? Did I try to drown Logan that day? A shudder ran through her. Am I that evil?

She met Logan's quizzical gaze and felt sick. "She wants you dead, Logan." she said. "That day on the dam—she wanted you dead. I remember her urging us into that leaky dingy... then I remember my father pulling you out of the water..." She shook her head. "But I don't remember..." She looked at Logan. "Did I try to drown you, Logan? Did I?" The sting of unshed tears burned her eyes.

Logan frowned.

"Paige, you were just a baby. It was a childish prank that went wrong. I couldn't swim. Forget it, but promise me you won't go to the house alone, okay? The rest we will deal with tomorrow."

Frustration surged through her and she shook her head. "I can't let it go, Logan. I need to remember... all of it.

"Tomorrow, Paige, not now. Go and get some rest."

She recognized the wisdom of his words and nodded agreement. "I will grab a room at the motor inn just on the other side of the parklands, if that makes you feel more comfortable. That will make it easy to come fetch you tomorrow."

He nodded ever so slightly. The movement made him wince, and he shut his eyes.

She laid a hand on his arm. "Rest, Logan. I will be back tomorrow..."

He forced his eyes open. They were filled with question as he sought assurance she would obey his instructions.

"No. I won't go into the house."

He gave a shadow of a smile. The action drew his wide mouth up into a lopsided curve that showed white, even teeth.

Paige stood fighting the desire to lean forward and kiss him lightly on the mouth. She wondered what his mouth would feel like caressing her own and what he would taste like. Would his taste be as intoxicating as his masculine scent was just after he had showered or when he had been working for a couple of hours and was bathed in good, fresh masculine perspiration. Without another word, she pulled herself out of her reverie and left the room. Lust came easy, but forgiveness did not for the man who destroyed her family.

Even in the austere blandness of the hotel room, sleep was elusive. She tossed and turned scolding herself for being so gullible as to be spooked by an old lady's mystical warning. Despite the burning exhaustion she finally gave in and turned on her tablet. She looked up the name Qarinah and found it was a demon or a ghost from old Arabic superstition or Arabian mythology. This type of ghost did indeed have sex with its chosen victim and sucked their life-force out of them. The article said these ghosts would also get angry and vengeful if their chosen one fell in love with another. Could the ghost hate Logan so much it intended to kill him? She searched farther and found plenty of anecdotal evidence of just that happening. Fear grew large and cold inside as long blocked memories stirred. Logan would be in trouble if he stayed at the house. Sickening trepidation washed through her followed closely by a prickling burn. She was in her own trouble—developing feelings for Logan Dunsford–Hamilton.

Finally she slept, but it was far from restful. Ghosts lurking on the edge of dreams filled with pioneers, the house, and vicious domestic abuse. All the time in the background she could hear the sound of a woman sobbing.

She woke as an ambulance screamed past then she slept again.

This time she heard her father's voice behind the door, angry and accusing—her mother crying and Sarah trying to soothe the situation. Her father's angry face, glared as it loomed huge in her dream—glared down at her with such contempt, such accusation, such fear she had shriveled before it. She grappled in her dream trying to capture the memory. What she had done to deserve such an expression? But the memory shimmied away and the dream faded.

It was almost light when she woke. Her eyes were tired and scratchy. Lethargy from lack of sleep held her heavy against the bed. She rolled over and burrowed back under the blankets. She didn't have to pick Logan up from hospital until eleven. It occurred to her that Tony and his boys would return to a deserted house. Would they work or walk? If so, what time. She snoozed on and off in a vague half consciousness.

The jangle of her phone jerked her wide awake. She peered out from under the quilt at her phone. It was Tony and the time was eight am.

"Hey, Bella, how is the boss?"

"I don't know, Tony. They kept him in last night."

"Okay. Do you think he would want us to continue with the work on the kitchen?"

Paige rolled over and laid her head back on the pillow. "To be honest, Tony, I don't know, but I would say yes. We want to get the extension to lock up before the winter."

Tony cleared his throat. "Okay, Bella, we'll get started on the one external wall he wants removed and the cladding on the two internals. Then tomorrow, we can dig the floor up and prepare the ground for the footings."

"Okay, Tony, just do what Logan has instructed you to do. He'll be back just after eleven."

***

Three hours later, Paige walked into the ward just in time to see Logan taking instructions from the doctor.

"All right, Doc. I will see I'm not alone for the next two or three days and yes, I will take it easy and get plenty of rest. Look. See? My minder has just arrived." He pointed at Paige, a wide grin lighting his face up under the two-day growth of beard.

She frowned back at him. "Logan, I'm..."

"My minder. Now, Doc, can I go?"

The doctor looked at Paige. "Now, you make sure he gets plenty of rest, and if he has any vision problems or severe headaches, you're to bring him back here straight away. Is that understood by both of you?"

Logan smiled.

Paige nodded. "Yes, Doctor. I will see he does all the right things." She held out the keys when they reached the car.

Logan shook his head. "You drive. I still have a headache."

Suddenly self-conscious, she slipped into the driver's seat and turned the key. She looked across at Logan leaning back in the passenger seat.

"Just drive, Paige. It's fully insured, and it is only a car." He didn't even open his eyes.

Holding her breath, she reversed out and headed back to the house.

With his eyes still closed, Logan asked, "Did Tony and his boys turn up this morning?"

"They did."

"I wondered if they would, considering Tony blames Joe for the accident. What're they working on?"

"Tony said you wanted one external wall out and the cladding from the two internals, so that is what he was going to do."

"Good. No sign of the tree lopper?"

"No, but Tony rang to say the stonemason guy had already made a start," she informed him, as she pulled into the drive.

Logan took the keys from Paige and headed inside. "I'll just grab a shower and a change of clothes."

Moments later, he swore loudly. A couple of loud thumps followed.

Paige went to investigate with Tony in her wake and found Logan struggling to turn the keys in the lock.

When they wouldn't turn he kicked the door. It rattled and vibrated under his onslaught, but would not budge. Logan kicked it again. "How could it have jammed so tight since yesterday?"

Tony glanced at the sky. "No rain, no swelling. Shall I get the jimmy bar?".

Logan nodded.

Paige took the keys from his unresisting hands.

He moved aside without being asked and leaned against the wall. His face was ashen under the bandages and his out-of-control stubble.

Paige slipped the key in the door, turned it, and pushed it open. She stepped through and turned, but as Logan went to follow her, the door

was wrenched savagely out of her hand and swung shut with a crash.

"Hey, what the hell?" She grabbed the lock, but the door was stuck fast. A warm enveloping sense of peace and love wrapped around her. She didn't want to open the door.

Logan thumped on the door. "Open the door. Are you all right, Paige?"

"Keep him out of my house—killer's spawn. Send him away—like you did before."

The words were a mere whisper, but distinct, in the slightest of British accents. Shivers tingled down the length of her spine. The voice sounded like her own, played back from a recording—but higher, disembodied, and more articulate.

"No, I will not." Paige grabbed the door handle. With her full weight thrown back she wrenched the door open. The sudden response tumbled her back against the wall. She still gripped the handle.

"What happened? Are you all right?" Logan stood swaying in the doorway.

She nodded, not quite sure she was.

"Tony, if you get onto the kitchen walls, I will be out in a minute." Logan headed for the bathroom.

"Logan, maybe you shouldn't go into the house. She does not want you here. The ghost wants me to send you away... like I did before."

Logan turned to face her. A frown furrowed his forehead. "You didn't send me away last time. It was my parents.

"Yes, but it was because of the 'accidents' caused by me."

He grinned. "I can swim now, so you can't drown me, but you could try in the shower if you like."

"Logan, it's not funny."

He frowned again. "What do you expect me to do? Run? I'm not scared of you, and I won't be scared off by some disembodied specter. This is our house and whatever she is, a ghost or a figment of our imagination, she's going to have to share or move out."

"But she almost killed you."

"Well, she's going to have to try harder then, because I'm not going to leave. Don't worry. It will be all right." He turned away.

Paige sighed. Even after the bricks, he still wasn't taking the risk seriously. She sighed again. And there was nothing she could do to protect him.

***

Logan was barely out of the shower when the tree lopper arrived, minutes in front of the materials for the new stonework. Logan inspected the progress being made on repairing the old stone and was pleased with the way the work was coming along. Within an hour, the tree lopper had taken half the tree down. Already there was more light in both the substitute kitchen and the dining room.

With so many workmen on site, Paige decided she would only get in the way, so she decided to look for the family tree, old papers, and diaries Martin promised Sarah had left in the house for her. She was interested in the family tree and, in particular, to find out just where Logan fitted in.

While she still held Logan accountable for her parents' divorce and was acutely aware of the residual bitterness that colored her opinion of him, she couldn't help but be attracted to him. That attraction scared her. She couldn't shake the feeling it was dangerous—for Logan.

It also worried her that Logan denied having a woman in his bed, especially after what the old lady at the hospital had said. Could the ghost be sucking his life force out through some form of deathly embrace? Surely Logan could tell the difference between a real woman and a specter. And if it was a real woman, it bothered Paige that Logan would lie or see the necessity to lie—they were not a couple, after all. Then again, if it was the ghost, she needed to know who she was and why she hated Logan so much. And for her own peace of mind she needed to remember what had happened when she was a child.

With a tremendous effort, she pushed her dark thoughts away, and proceeded to search, but when her search of each room only turned up a couple of journals she decided to brave the attic. The pull-down stairs seemed steady enough, but she climbed cautiously. The attic was dusty and dark, with spider webs hanging in lace curtains across the dirty windows and in the corners of the room. The low-roofed space was filled with boxes and trunks, discarded toys, and unidentified items.

She was keen to delve farther into Sarah Hamilton's world. While her recent journals had proven fascinating, she was disappointed they only went back for the last five years of her life. She hoped to find more journals, ones that would help her piece together the puzzle of the ghost and its dislike of Logan, and just why Logan was entitled to the bequest in the first place.

Each container revealed dusty, discarded items that would prove interesting fossicking later, but today she was on a mission. Halfway through exploring the jumbled collection of items, her throat was so dry and scratchy she couldn't stop coughing, and decided it was time for a coffee break.

A movement in her peripheral vision sparked needles of apprehension. She turned. The ghost was sitting on one of the trunks. Just as she remembered her. But in that moment awareness sparked—she looked so much like her they could have been sisters. A sulky expression marred the ghost's delicate features. Malevolence emanated from the apparition. It slid over Paige's skin with an icy chill.

"Get him out of my house, Daughter—like you did before. This house is yours, only yours. Get the killer's spawn out of my house."

Paige stared at the vision. The words whispered in her head. Like she had before? She shook her head. She had no idea what the ghost meant. "I have no idea what you mean."

The specter frowned. "Remove him, Daughter. You must."

Apprehension washed over her. Frightened for the first time Paige slammed the trunk shut, turned and shuffled toward the trapdoor. As her foot touched the first steps a weight shoved against her shoulder. She clung to the rope handrails, swayed then steadied. Paige took two more steps down. A sharp scrape echoed against the walls. She looked up. The diffused light from the attic windows was blocked. A trunk filled the trapdoor opening. It loomed above her for a long moment. Paige scrabbled down the steps. The pull down steps shuddered. The weight of the falling trunk slammed into her back, swiping her feet from under her. The floor filled her vision as she hurtled toward it. She hit with a thud. The air in her lungs whooshed out with a painful forced expulsion, and she grunted in pain as the trunk crashed to the floor right beside her.

"You will remove him from my house, Daughter. You will."

Paige rolled over and peered up into the gloominess of the attic, but the ghost had gone. She assessed the damage to her body before she made any attempt to get up. Damn bitch could have killed me. What the fuck does she think this is? Everything hurt, but nothing excruciatingly, except for the sudden memory stabbing though her brain. This had happened before, only it wasn't her that had been pushed last time. Tears started in her eyes.

Footsteps thudded up the passage.

"Good grief, Paige. Are you all right?" Logan knelt beside her.

Tony stood behind him, the first-aid kit dangling from his hand.

She moved her limbs tentatively. "Yes, I think I'm okay." Her words faded as the tears began to fall. "Logan, she pushed me."

He helped her stand. "You're lucky you didn't break something, falling like that."

She clung to him as the memory of another time flickered through her mind. She felt sick.

"Come outside and sit in the fresh air for a while. You sure you don't need a doctor?"

She shook her head. "No, I'm fine and look, Sarah's journals—lots of them." She bent to retrieve one.

"Leave them for now." He took her arm. "Come, sit for a moment."

Despite the fact that she was fine she followed him outside. "Really I'm fine just a bit shaken and a lot better than you, by the look of it."

His face was haggard and pale.

"Logan, you need to rest. Now!"

"Okay, okay, but not in the house. I'm going to take a nap in the car out on the street. It's too noisy here."

Paige suspected that wasn't the only reason he was going out to the car, but she didn't say anything.

She went and lay down for a while, but rest was impossible with the sound of Tony's digger as it growled and rumbled through the house. Paige began to wish she had gone with Logan and decided a coffee might help. While she waited for the kettle to boil, the gutsy roar of the digger faded to a low growl. Before Paige could exit the house to see if Tony was going to stop for smoko silence enveloped her.

Tony had cut the engine of the digger, the scoop of his digger half in the soil and half out. As Tony jumped to the ground, Paige hurried towards the stalled digger, pessimistic that Tony had cut a water pipe or something similar, despite the carefully drawn plans.

"Call Logan, Bella. Get him here quick."

"What is it, Tony?"

The dark haired Italian shook his head. "This is not for your eyes, Bella. Get Logan pronto."

She called Logan on the mobile. He sounded sleepy when he first answered.

"Yep."

"Tony needs..."

"Holy shit." The frantic bellow was scratchy through the device.

"Logan?"

Silence, then an ear shattering screech and bone rattling crunch.

"Logan... answer me. What's happened? Logan, are you all right?" Paige was already moving toward the street. "Tony, something's happened." She waved the waiting contractor forward.

The two of them ran down the driveway and into the street. Logan's car was nowhere to be seen. Paige looked up and down the street then turned downward.

She froze. Her breath caught in her chest.

Tony ran passed her, mumbling through his panting breath. "Mamma mia! The boss's been killed. Mamma mia! The car is smashed."

Paige forced her legs to take the steps needed to reach the red car, now wedged into the neighbor's garage roller door. The bent metal of the roller door was wrapped around the bonnet of the car. The driver's door of the car was open.

Tony smiled as she approached. "He is all good, Bella. Do not worry. The car..." Tony waved his hands in gesture of surrender. "The car... she is not so good."

"Logan?"

He looked up at her. "I'm a bit shook up, but okay. No further injuries. The car didn't get up enough speed before it hit the door—like last time, when it hit the gatepost." He looked rueful.

Paige looked at him for a moment then comprehension came. They both burst out laughing at the same time.

Paige sobered first. "I didn't do it."

Logan pushed himself out of the seat, looked over the damage then turned to Paige.

"I know, Paige. Either I bumped the park brake while I slept or your ghost is at work again."

Tony returned from hammering on the neighbors' front door.

"They're all out, Boss. Better leave a note." The contractor handed over some paper and a chewed on his pencil. "We have more important things to do—up at the house."

With the note written, they walked slowly back to the house. Tony refused to talk about 'the problem'.

***

Once at the house, Tony insisted Paige stay back as he and Logan approached the digger.

Logan wondered what was so terrible that Tony refused to let Paige see.

Logan looked down in the hole, and gasped. The white pieces that sprinkled the tumble of red dirt stood out starkly. They looked like bones—human bones. As Logan knelt down to peer more closely at the foreign matter, a savage swirl of wind whipped up around him, spinning dirt, grit, grass, and leaves in a viciously fast moving whirl-wind.

Tony backed away, his arm up to shelter his face from the abrasive debris. "Holy Mother of God, what is this... this wind?"

"Logan?" Paige called.

He heard Paige's voice, as if from a distance, while the wind roared in his ears and the debris it carried slapped and sliced at his face and hands.

"Killer's spawn, leave me rest in peace." The wind battered at him, dragging him away from the kitchen.

"Leave me in peace. Haven't you done enough?" The voice screeched above the wind as it became a chant. "Killer's spawn, killer's spawn."

The words echoed over and over, piercing Logan's hearing, until his brain cringed against the ungodly intrusion in his head. He stumbled, lost his footing, and fell. He hit the ground hard, but was free of the spinning dust tornado. Paige was there. His ears hurt so much he could hardly make out what she was saying.

"Are you all right?"

He nodded and climbed unsteadily to his feet. "Is everyone okay?"

"I'm fine. It was only you that was... that was attacked."

"This damn house is going to be the death of me. I am beginning to wonder just what that old lady had in mind when she set the terms of her will."

"Oh, come on, Logan, surely you don't think Sarah was up to something untoward?"

"I am beginning to wonder."

Logan walked back over to where Tony was kneeling on the ground by the scoop of the digger. In his hand was a human skull.

Logan wiped the dirt out of his eyes. "Hell, what do we do now?"

Paige touched his back as she leaned over to see. Her warm breath tickled on the side of his face and her perfume wafted tantalizingly under his nose.

"Is this our ghost?"

"Probably—and if no official death has been recorded on this property, it means it was probably foul play. I'd better call the cops."

As he dialed, he had visions of all sorts of delays while they exhumed the bones and identified them. The property would become a crime scene. Damn, damn, damn. This was the last thing he needed.

Paige fidgeted beside him. "This is exciting. We can find out who it is perhaps and maybe they'll be able to rest in peace."

"And maybe we can find out why she hates me so much."

"Maybe."

The sound of sobbing was soft and mournful. It wrapped itself around them as they all stood silently around the jumble of bones that had once been a person. As the sobbing turned to wailing, Tony covered his ears.

"Sorry, Logan. I'm not working with the dead wailing in my ears. Me and the boys will be in the pub when you've got rid of that monstrosity."

Logan nodded. He'd expected it. Tony made no secret of the fact he was superstitious.

"I'll give you a call, Tony, when it's all sorted."

He stood side by side with Paige and stared down at the skeleton, only the soft sobbing intruded on the silence.

The police were efficient in examining the scene and taping off the kitchen area. They covered the site to preserve the bones, promising a forensic pathologist would be out the next day to make the necessary examination.

It was late before they left, and Logan was again feeling the effects of his cracked head.

"I'm going to turn in Paige. I'm beat."

"Night, Logan. Just try to keep your activities down to a dull roar tonight or better still, forgo it altogether. You really aren't up to it."

He frowned. "I see you still don't believe me. But I assure you that I sleep alone and have every night since I moved into the house—actually every night since I caught my wife in bed with my best friend." He smiled now. "You are most welcome to join me though, if you want to?"

Chapter Five

The heat rushed into her face and she dropped her gaze to the floor. Damn, it was so tempting. He was an attractive man, and she liked him. He had made no secret of his awareness of her, but she held back by the jumbled memories of the past. She had always blamed Logan and his lies for the breakup of her family. But as she made sense of the fractured memories she had doubts that he was the cause of her greatest hurt.

That she had tried to hurt him when they were children changed everything. Guilt burned through her. That, and the fear she might try to hurt him again if she came under the influence of the ghost kept her from accepting his casual offer. Besides, she figured if he was really interested he would have made some effort to actually seduce her. Not wanting to explain all this to him, she just smiled and said, "Thanks, Logan, but I wouldn't want to cramp your dream lover's style."

Immediate disappointment swept across his face at her rejection, and she felt flustered for a moment. She did want him, but she didn't really want to be one of a harem.

"Night, Paige."

"Good night, Logan." With dark resolution she closed her bedroom door on temptation.

***

She opened her eyes to total darkness and knew immediately what had woken her. The sound of sex—loud, enthusiastic sex, in the room across the passage.

She rolled over and pulled the pillow over her head. She was tired. She wanted to sleep, but her pussy was reacting to the sounds. It wanted to be stroked and filled. She couldn't banish the picture in her head of his cock—its length and thickness—and imagining how it would feel thrusting into her. Filling her. "Damn you, Logan," she muttered. She rolled over again. "Shut up, for goodness sake. Shut up!" The noise from the other room continued unabated. Fury whipped over her. It was the height of bad manners, not to be just a little discreet, especially after he had invited her into his bed. She piled out of bed, and not bothering to pull on her wrap, she stalked across the passage.

Without knocking, she flung open the door and barged in. "For God's sake, you two, give it a rest. I want to sleep..."

Her angry shout died in her throat. Logan lay naked on the bed, his cock erect as he thrust into the air. His hips were thrusting up and down. His balls were jiggling. His hands clutched the sheet in a white knuckled grip, and his face and chest were bathed in sweat. Paige stared.

A light mist formed over Logan's naked, thrusting body. It took form. It was a woman. It was her ghost. Paige screamed then, for this misty specter could have been her. She could see where his engorged cock was thrusting with a desperate rhythm into the misty form, right where her pussy would have been. The apparition was riding him in a violent bounce, pounding down on his cock.

On his exposed chest sat the big cat. It was kneading the skin of his chest with savage punches. The sharp claws ripped the exposed flesh open in long gashes. Cat glared at her. Hissed. Golden eyes were slits in the darkness. Paige stood rooted to the spot. She tried to speak, to scream again, but nothing would come out of her struggling convulsing throat.

She jumped forward, both hands in front of her, and slapped at the air in front of the cat.

It stopped kneading and stood up. It's back arched up. The red fur stood straight out. Its tail was straight and stiff in the air. Cat bared its teeth and hissed.

Paige kept going. "Get off him, Cat! Leave him alone! Logan, wake up."

The misty shape of the female apparition began to disperse, but Logan kept thrusting.

Paige slapped at the cat.

The ginger fiend swiped back, all claws extended.

Paige drew back out of range then picked up Logan's belt from the floor. She whipped the air so the belt whistled right past the cat's ears.

It stopped attacking Logan's chest and turned towards her, crouched, spat, and showed its teeth.

Paige paused then swung the belt again.

The cat sprang at that moment.

She backed off, but the cat landed on her chest.

The back feet clawed her breasts. The front feet reached over her shoulder and opened up the skin in eight deep gashes. It teeth were right in her face. She pulled her head back and screamed, again and again. She beat at the cat with open hands.

The enraged animal finally retracted its claws, dropped to the floor, and stalked out of the room, its tail straight up in the air. Nausea gurgled in her gut as her legs sagged, and she crumpled to the floor. The scratches burned like fire, and she could feel warm blood running down her breasts.

Logan was lying now on his side, moaning and shaking.

The ghost loomed over him. She pointed a finger at Paige. "Daughter, go from here. Do not interfere with what must be. Go now, or you shall die along with the killer's spawn."

Paige faced the naked ghost. "You will not kill him. I will not let you."

The specter cackled then. "You cannot stop me, Daughter. I do not need your help this time." The ghost laughed again and in a swirl of mist was gone.

Paige turned back to Logan.

He continued to moan as he lay semi-conscious on the bed. His hand enclosed his cock, which was still erect. He pumped the shaft in a desperate rhythm, and his hips still thrust.

Paige watched him not sure what to do. It was obvious Logan was under some sort of spell, as he seemed asleep but was not.

His eyes were wide open and staring, but somehow sightless.

Logan's desperation to climax was obvious in his thrusting. His cock was wet with fluids. When he groaned, the sound had such an edge of desperation that Paige knew what she needed to do. Already on her knees Paige slid forward on the floor, until she was next to the bed. She reached out, and wrapped her hand around his hot flesh immediately moving with the same rhythm as his own hand, until she could unclasp his fingers and replace his with hers. Then she moved her hand up and down the shaft, using the fluids to lubricate her movements. With her other hand, she cupped his balls and rolled them gently around. He groaned again, but it sounded less tortured this time. She ran her fingers under the head of his penis and up the small groove as she tightened her hold on the shaft and pumped hard and fast. Her other hand alternatively played with his balls.

He moaned loudly as he thrust faster, his climax rippled along the shaft, and seconds later he spurted cum in thick, white streams onto the sheets.

She ran her hand firmly down the length of the shaft, right to the end as each spurt came, and continued when it ceased, milking his cock for every last drop. He moaned at each manipulation before he sagged back on the bed, his cock now soft in her hand. She let it slip free.

He blinked a couple of times and asked faintly, "Why are you here Paige?"

"I'm here to save you from the ghost."

"'The ghost? Where's the ghost?"

"She's gone, for now." Paige glanced around the room to confirm she was gone.

Logan put his hand to his forehead. "Oh fuck, I feel awful. Paige. You're bleeding."

"Yes, so are you."

"What... what the hell happened?"

Paige shook her head. "You tell me, Logan."

He shut his eyes for a moment then opened them and looked up at her.

"She came... I had another dream. This woman comes and we have sex—ever since I've been in the house. Good sex—damn mind blowing sex. But, tonight was different... like she wanted to hurt me... or drive me insane..." He shook his head as his words lost coherence.

"Get up and put some clothes on. We both need medical attention."

He looked up at her, then down at the blood still seeping from the scratches on his chest and abdomen. "What happened?"

"A feral cat got in the house and attacked you. A big ginger feral cat. When I tried to scare it off, it attacked me."

He shook his head. "That's not what I remember. I remember…" He suddenly fell silent, then he looked directly into her eyes. "I remember the relief of finally being able to come…"

She stared hard back at him. "You remember being attacked by a feral cat."

He started to shake his head.

She reached out and gripped his shoulder. "Yes, Logan. We were both attacked by a feral cat."

He looked at her, his gaze intent and probing, but without another word he pushed himself into a sitting position. "Oh shit." He suddenly realized he was naked and messy with cum. He went to pull the sheet over his now soft cock.

"Don't bother, I've already seen all there is to see. Just put these on while I get something to stem the bleeding." He cleared his throat as he took the boxer briefs and jeans she held out to him, but he didn't look up at her. She couldn't see his face, but she thought it might be slightly colored.

When she got back from raiding the first-aid kit, he was still sitting on the bed.

"Logan, get dressed."

He looked up at her. His expression was vague and confused, but he pulled on his boxer briefs and jeans, although the fly was still unzipped. She took a couple of large dressings out of their wrappers and pressed them against Logan's taut abdomen, and he held them in place until she had applied some tape to secure them. The scratches were still bleeding quite heavily.

She'd pulled on some three-quarter pants and a tee on the way back. Her shoulder was burning with pain and she could feel the warm wetness of her blood as it seeped out and slid down her breasts and abdomen. With shaky hands she wiped up the worst of the blood and pressed the dressings to the deeper scratches. She handed him the tape. His fingers were cold as he pressed the dressings against the wounds and taped them in placed with the pieces of tape she broke off for him. She flinched at his ministrations, even though they were gentle and brief.

He laid his hand on her uninjured shoulder. "They look nasty. Are you going to be okay?"

She nodded, but was fighting tears now, as the shock of what she had seen and the sudden frenzied attack by the cat chilled her to the bone. She pulled her bloodied tee back down and carefully slipped on a light jacket.

Logan pulled on one of his button through shirts, but left it open. He picked up a the light blanket from the end of his bed and wrapped it around her and together they hobbled out to the car.

"Hang in there. It won't take long to get down to the Emergency Department. We both need stitches, I think."

She couldn't stop shaking now. Wave after wave of trembling rushed over her. Logan helped her into the passenger seat then slid in beside her.

It was a long wait at the Emergency Department, but finally they were attended to. Paige could see the skepticism in the doctor's face as he stitched their wounds, and he asked several times if they wished to speak to the police. Finally, as he dressed Paige's abdomen, he grudgingly accepted their explanation that a feral cat had inflicted the wounds and suggested they get an officer of the RSPCA or the local council to come and remove it.

The sky was lightening as they left the hospital. The silence was thick between them. Paige didn't know how to start the conversation or how much to say. She didn't want Logan to feel embarrassed by what she'd done. Actually, she hoped he wasn't fully aware she had been the one who brought him to a heaving climax. As she stared at the road ahead, she wondered what it would be like to have Logan thrusting into her pussy with his large, hard cock. She didn't even try to deny she was extremely attracted to the man driving in silence beside her.

To witness him thrusting hard and fast into an ethereal entity had been a real turn on. As for the ethereal entity, that worried her. The old woman's warning poked at the back of her mind. She struggled to get her head around the thought that a ghost could have sex with a living being, and draw their life force out, even though she knew it was possible from her research. Knowing it was one thing but seeing it was quite another.

Logan admitted it had been going on for some nights, and it was obvious that he was nowhere near the previous robust condition he'd displayed before moving into the house. At least she knew now he hadn't been lying to her about his sexual companion, and she even felt a little guilty for thinking he had. She worried how he could be protected from the ghost's assaults. Would he have to move from the house to be safe, therefore causing both of them to forfeit their inheritance?

The paranormal had never really worried her before—she accepted her physic ability, but had chosen never to develop it. Now she wished she had. No matter which angle she looked at the events of the last couple of days, she could not make sense of them.

The house was cold, dark and silent.

"I'm going to get some sleep, Logan. Can we cancel Tony and his crew for today?"

Logan looked down at her. "No need, it's Sunday."

She nodded and turned away from him. As she opened her door, she sensed his presence by her side.

"Paige?"

She turned to him and a wave of sympathy flooded through her as she took in his grey, haggard face, the stitched slashes showing through the waterproof dressings on his chest, and the look of uncertainty on his face.

"I don't think I can sleep in my room... I'm... I don't want... God damn it, Paige, I'm scared she is going to come back... that this time she'll drive me over the edge. I don't want to sleep alone."

"Oh, Logan." She was well aware he was attracted to her, and she believed he remembered her hand job, so for a fleeting moment she wondered if it was a ploy to get into her bed or a genuine concern for his own safety. The look on his face was enough to allay any concerns she had.

"I promise I won't try to take advantage of you. I just want company..."

She reached out and took his cold hand in her grasp and led him into her room. Self-consciousness was sharp between them as Paige undressed. Logan took his jeans off but left his boxer briefs on. They climbed into bed and snuggled in under the duvet. They lay side by side, not touching, as both of them stared up at the ceiling.

"Thank you, for saving me tonight and letting me sleep in your bed. I know I'm being pathetic, but for some reason, my nocturnal dreams are playing havoc with my mind and my body. It has gotten to the stage I can't cope with it anymore, and I'm beginning to believe there might be something to that old woman's ranting. I would never have admitted it before, but I think I am being haunted by something less than human."

She turned and wriggled to close the space between their semi-naked bodies. She laid a hand on his arm. "I'm convinced you are being haunted. I saw the figure of a woman astride you. Both of you were going hammer and tongs. I think though, I was more shocked by the cat. Its attack on your chest, and then me, was really savage. I did read on the net that household pets can be associated with a spirit like this one. The cat always seems to be around when she is."

"Yes, Cat seems to be with her each time she does something. Any time anything happens that damn cat is there. But why, Paige... why the assaults?"

"I don't know, but there are plenty of stories on the net about people experiencing the same thing. We need to put a stop to it. You'll not survive twelve months here in the house at this rate. Look at your-self—you're tired, fatigued, have headaches, and physical injuries you can't explain. Despite the fact I don't want to give up this inheritance, I will understand if you choose to."

He adjusted his position and slipped his closest arm under her good shoulder and drew her close. "I don't want to lose it either, but I suspect you're right. I will not be alive to collect it if I stay and this vendetta against me continues."

"Did you really enjoy the sex?"

He chuckled. "I did, at first. It was so real. She's so beautiful and sexually skilled, but there was something missing after the first time—I can't explain the difference. The last time was actually unpleasant. She seemed cruel. I couldn't come, even though I desperately needed to. It was as though she was preventing me. Trying to drive me insane..."

He lifted himself slightly and leaned towards her. When his lips touched hers, the heat between them sizzled. Each spot where their skin touched was a smoldering ember just waiting to be fanned into life. The pressure of his mouth was firm and controlled, as he explored every inch of her lips. The taste of him was unique—mellow—like a rich red wine.

Then he pulled away. "Thank you, Paige, for what you did. You brought me back from the brink of madness. Now, sleep while I hold you. We will keep each other safe from marauding ghosts."

***

Logan slept on as she slipped out of the bed. He'd kept his word and made no attempt to seduce her. She suspected that was more from his physical condition than good manners. She was almost disgruntled, but pleased, too, that he was a man of his word. Each day he seemed to be proving himself trustworthy in her estimation. Maybe the blame she laid at his door for causing her parents' break up was skewed. She knew her memories weren't clear about that terrible time in her life.

Making as little noise as possible, she slipped on some clothes and gathered up her drawing pad and pastels. She loved to draw and paint—not that she considered herself an artist, but it was relaxing. Today though, she wasn't looking to relax. Today she wanted to produce a likeness from memory. The afternoon sun was warm on the front veranda. She left the doors open so she could still see Logan—just in case he had a visitor.

With practiced strokes, she outlined the face as she remembered it—the long, flowing strawberry hair, small shapely mouth, blue eyes, and heart-shaped face. When she thought it was as accurate as she could make it, she worked on another—a full portrait. To the naked figure she added garments—a tight bodice with a high neckline, full and flowing long skirt, and a bonnet. She drew the hair in ringlets. She stared at what she had drawn, not sure whether to be awed or angry. She held in her hands two portraits—both so like herself. Bitter disappointment scratched at her as she wondered how she could have got it so wrong. The more she looked though, the more the drawings looked like the specter she had seen attacking Logan.

She heard him pad up behind her and she turned around. "So, what do you think?"

"That's her... that's my dream lover, but.... but Paige, it does so look like you."

She sighed. "I know—somehow I got it wrong. I wasn't trying for a self-portrait..."

"They're not self-portraits. It's her. There are differences... See, her mouth is smaller than yours, her eyes more heavy lidded, and the eyebrows thicker, more arched..." He pointed to the drawings' subtle lines.

"That could just be my dodgy drawing."

"No. It's her, but I would say you two could be sisters or..."

"She could be my ancestor... Hey, maybe there is something in all those journals in the trunk I found in the attic. I was going to ask you to help me get the other trunks down. I suspect the other trunks also have journals in them. Do you feel up to bringing down one of the boxes of journals?" She indicated his chest.

Logan stood and stretched. "No problems, but I might need some help down the stairs. They're a bit rickety."

"You trust me to help you with the steps—after what I did before?"

He grinned. "I'll make you come down first. That way you can't push me."

Her smile faded. She felt consumed with guilt.

He frowned. "Hey, I was joking."

She gave him a sad smile. "Maybe you should take it all a bit more seriously. I did push you. I could have killed you."

"But you didn't. Let it go. Come on the day is a wasting."

***

Once showered, dressed, and revived with hot coffee, they headed to the attic to get the journals.

Logan went to pull the stairs down then turned back to her. "You could have killed me several times when we were little. In fact I'm surprised you didn't, but I am not afraid of you anymore. I don't think it was because you were inherently evil. I think it was something else. Now, up you go. Show me which one."

It took a while to determine the dates because Paige had decided she wanted the oldest ones first. They were both covered in dust and spider webs by the time they figured out which box they needed and climbed awkwardly down the stairs.

"That's it for today. I will get the rest when I'm healed. Quite a bit of bedtime reading in that lot anyway. I..." His words faded as he stared in fascination and trepidation. "Paige..."

"Yes?"

"You have a companion... right behind you." His voice cracked as he pointed at the spirit.

Paige looked over her shoulder. Shrouded in mist, but clear enough for Paige to jump back. A reflection of herself almost—or her portraits—only this woman had blue eyes. Her hair was the same color as Paige's natural color but was long and curled into ringlets under a delicate lace cap. As Paige locked gazes with the apparition, it smiled—a tender smile filled with love. Then tears slid slowly down the ghostly cheeks. A churning mixture of emotions rushed through Paige, as stunned into frozen immobility for a long moment, she stared, speechless. As the apparition moved toward her, she jumped back, straight into Logan's embrace. He closed his arms tightly around her.

"Is she going to hurt us?"

The ghost's expression changed to one of hatred. The temperature of the air dropped dramatically as misty fingers reached out to them. The icy strands insidiously forced their way between them, leaving freezing trails along their skin where it was in contact.

Paige felt the icy burn and instinctively moved out of Logan's embrace.

The specter smiled as she raised her arms and pushed toward Logan.

He flew backward with an undignified grunt, as the air was forced out of his lungs by the violence of his landing.

"Killer's spawn—leave my house."

Logan scrambled to his feet. "It's my house, damn you... mine... ours."

Paige felt the air rush past her and Logan stumbled backwards again, falling against the door frame.

"Stop it," Paige screamed at the apparition.

The ghost looked at her and shook her head. "My house, our house—he must leave." She disintegrated into nothing. "Leave me to rest." The high pitched wail from the darkness of the attic expanse above them scraped along Paige's nerves.

Paige helped Logan to his feet and wrapped her arms around his waist.

"God damn it, what has she got against me? She likes you—all smiles and tender glances..."

"Maybe one of your ancestors upset her. I mean, if it is her skeleton we found, maybe someone murdered her. Maybe that someone has something to do with you."

"Why take it out on me?"

She pulled out of his embrace. "Maybe, she doesn't realize how long it's been since she died. They say that those on the other side or trapped here, have no concept of time. It's possible she thinks you are the son of her killer, not the five times removed grandson..."

"Are you saying my five times removed grandfather or one of my other ancestors murdered her?"

She shrugged. "Not exactly, Logan, but you get my drift. Someone in the past is guilty and they may have a connection to you."

"But we are related. We have the same five times removed grandfather, William Dunsford don't we? So what is the solution? Other than me moving out and both of us forfeiting the inheritance?"

"I don't know, but every moment you are in the house you're risking your life. Is this inheritance worth it?"

"Well, I'm not going to leave."

"In that case you will just have to be vigilant and I'll get busy doing some research to see what I can come up with."

"Okay. So what about going out for a quiet dinner? Get away from this house for a while."

"Sounds great. First dibs on the shower." She turned and ran up the passage giggling as she went.

Logan was right behind her. They barged through the bathroom door together. Moments later, they were entangled in the shower curtain. Logan grabbed her shoulders to steady her and she wrapped her arms around his neck and pulled his face down to hers. His mouth was firm, but silken smooth. Just the slightest of stubble rubbed her cheek as she covered his half-open mouth with hers. He stiffened for a moment then relaxed and wrapped his arms around her waist before cupping her buttocks to pull her hard against him.

She explored his mouth, tasting him by dipping her tongue between his lips. He met her tongue with a thrust of his own but he allowed hers to dominate his for a moment in a sensuous tussle. Then she pressed her mouth harder on his before she pulled away. He was still leaning towards her and looked a little disconcerted with the parting of their mouths. She made a snap decision—she wanted this man.

"Perhaps, we could save time and water by sharing."

Her hands were already reaching for his jean's stud and fly and with a wriggle of his slim hips, the denim dropped around his ankles. His black trunks clung to every outline of his body and the hardness of his cock lay like a thick, long rod against his thigh. She ran her hand over the cloth, lightly squeezing his shaft. She heard his indrawn breath as his hands fumbled with her shirt buttons.

They popped open, one at a time in quick succession, before he pushed her shirt apart to reveal her breasts. Cupping them with his hands Logan lowered his head to kiss the swell of her cleavage. Paige moaned as he trailed his tongue over their soft curves before he took a small pink nipple in his mouth. He flicked his tongue over its tip then suckled on the erect nub. Sparks fired right through her body as she felt him nibble gently with his teeth on the tender protrusion of flesh.

Logan brought his mouth back to hers as his hands fumbled with her shorts, before pushing the thin material down over her thighs, taking her panties with them. She was naked. He caressed her body with eager hands–her buttocks, breasts and back. He was careful of her injuries, as she was of his. Then still covering her mouth with his, and one hand cupping her right breast while his thumb still teased the nipple, he reached in and turned on the shower.

She tugged his boxer briefs down over his ass and eased his throbbing cock out of its enclosure. It felt hot and hard, the tip already damp. Released, it stood out straight from his body, the head glistening pink and wet. She ran her hand along the length and eased her circled fingers over the head, squeezing slightly.

He moaned.

With the water adjusted, he lifted her from the floor into the shower. The water sluiced over her body as he brushed the hair from her face, and took command of her mouth.

He cupped her butt cheeks and lifted her.

She felt his cock pressing against her abdomen and reached down to cup his balls. They hung low with a slight sprinkling of hair. She rolled them gently between her fingers. He parted his legs slightly. She cupped his balls completely in one hand and with the other stroked the hot skin between his legs.

Logan caressed her wet body then reached for the shower gel. Moments later, a delicately scented froth blossomed on her wet skin easing the passage of his hands as he brought them up to cup her breasts. Then he slid them down and dipped between her legs.

Like him, she parted her legs to give him unrestricted access. Her body throbbed. She could feel the bubbles against her sensitive skin, as he caressed her outer lips.

Then he carefully parted her lips and explored her inner flesh. Gently squeezing and rubbing he explored each fold.

As he found her clit, she gasped pressing toward him as he clasped it gently caressing up and down the erect little shaft then circled its base before dipping into her pussy. She pressed down towards where his finger was inserted, causing a wildfire to explode inside her, scorching her with waves of sensation.

Her response must have encouraged him and he quickened the thrusting and the pressure on her nub of pleasure.

A raging unexpected climax bunched in her pussy, crouched at her very center then burst through her core, her abdomen, and down her legs. She felt her knees weaken as she moaned her release against his mouth. Her pussy clenched and unclenched and she pushed down hard against his hand.

He held firm, not touching her clit as she came, but kept moving his finger deep inside her. Twisting and turning until she collapsed and softened as her climax dissipated.

Even as she moaned with aftershocks, he released her mouth and turned her to face the tiles. She leaned against them, glad of the support and let Logan run his hands up and down her body, soothing the fire, but at the same time, fanning the embers. His hands reached around and cupped her breasts as he kissed the neck and good shoulder through the flow of water. He slipped his hand between her legs into the folds of her lips and into her pussy. Perhaps three fingers this time, slid in and out.

She parted her legs and he increased the depth and spread with each thrust. The ache of sexual tension immediately began again in her pussy, where his fingers were thrusting. His other hand was caressing her clit, fleeting whisper soft flicks of his finger over the head. She almost scrunched down as the heat of desire bubbled and roiled through her. Her pussy clenched and tightened and she moaned against the cool water-washed tiles.

Logan removed his fingers and pressed his body against hers. His hands carefully opened her lips from between her legs.

The hot tip of his cock just rested at the opening of her pussy. She almost screamed with the need to feel him sink his cock into her. "For goodness sake, Logan, take me."

He chuckled. Then his cock slid into her—just the head filling her opening.

Then it was gone. Her body throbbed in protest, her pussy clenched, almost as if it could reach out and grab his cock and drag it into her. Then she felt it again. Just the head pressed into her hot, wet flesh. She moaned and pushed her body down, but Logan had control. Again he withdrew and then pressed in again. Her legs trembled. She wanted him so badly her climax simmering, just out of reach. All she would need is one thrust to explode.

His hands now held her waist. In fact he was practically holding her upright. He leaned down and trailed kisses along her neck as he pushed his throbbing cock in a little farther.

"Logan, please?"

He withdrew, not completely, but just so the head of his cock was stretching her opening. She stilled in expectation of the penetration she wanted so desperately. Every bit of her body tingled and trembled on the cusp of release. Her body cried out for that deep penetration. Then it came.

With a single thrust, Logan sank deep into her then partially withdrew and thrust again and again. She felt his large cock stretching her pussy.

She pressed back against his thrusts, embedding the length of his organ to the hilt inside her. Then she was gone. Her body exploded, shaking and aching, as the sensation of release roared through her like white hot lava. Her pussy clenched and relaxed and clenched again then she felt it tighten even more in response to enormous explosion in her pelvis as fluid squirted out around his cock when it thumped into her body. Her nails scraped the tiles and her legs shook. He held her around the waist as she gasped for breath. She was flying, but nothing mattered except the feel of his cock penetrating her.

Logan groaned and buried himself deep inside before he stilled. Then he moved again sending frissons of mellow sensations rolling over her. She felt his cockhead pressed against her cervix and the hot squirt of fluids filling her dripping pussy. His last few, gentler, thrusts pushed it out to run down her thighs and be washed away. She clung to the wall.

He clung to her his chest heaving. His cock still throbbed slightly inside her, but it was softening now and he let it slide out.

The action almost sent her into another spin.

He held her clutched to his chest now, letting the warm water sluice over both of them. Then he applied a small handful of bubbles to her mound and slid tenderly between her legs as he washed away his cum and her own juices.

It was so exquisite that she could not hold back the moan that escaped.

He chuckled and turned her before he frothed her hands. She knew what he wanted, and she reached out and rubbed his cock and balls with infinite gentleness.

His cock was still semi-hard and it was tempting to continue with her caressing until it was hard again, but she resisted. All she really wanted at this moment was to savor the most exquisite orgasm she had ever had.

He took control of her mouth and drank deeply from her moisture before he sucked on her tongue, and nibbled at her bottom lip. He reached up and turned the water off then he gently pushed her out of the shower alcove. He wrapped a huge, fluffy towel around her before hanging another around his hips. He lifted her face up and kissed her lightly and quickly.

"Mind blowing." His words were just a whisper against her mouth before he pulled away. "Time for dinner, my little ghost hunter." And he swept her up into his arms and carried her to her room.

After he left to dress, she stood for a long moment where he had placed her and hugged the towel tightly around her freshly washed body. She replayed their sexual exchange in her head. Her body immediately responded with a buzz of awareness and she knew with certainty she was eager to do it again—no matter the past still lingering in her mind and the consequences the ghost might administer.

***

In the quaint pub in a nearby hill town, they settled at a table by the open wood fire and placed their orders. Paige pulled out the pictures she had drawn and laid them on the table.

"It's definitely her. All we have to do is find out who she is."

"And why she hates me," Logan muttered, his expression one of rueful sadness.

She laid her hand over his. "Never mind."

"Do you think she will mind that we have... made love?"

"I don't know. I suppose we will find out tonight."

"Yeah, right. Great."

Paige laughed then. "Don't look so mournful. Isn't it every man's dream to have two women fighting over him? Both of them mad for his gorgeous body."

He laughed then, and leaned over the table to kiss her on the mouth. "Two live women maybe..."

Their meal came and they chatted about the renovations for a while and Logan promised to call the police to see when they could continue the kitchen additions.

"Tomorrow, I'm going to go to the city library to do some research on the women associated with the house and its history."

"I might do some work in the garden and make some plans for the landscaping. It would be nice to have it done before winter sets in," Logan said.

Paige sensed his edginess about being alone in the house. She understood his concerns, especially now she had a vested interest in more than their joint inheritance.

He put his arm around her shoulders as they left the warmth of the pub and strolled down the cold, moonlit street. She cuddled into his side.

"Tomorrow, if you have any trouble from her, just get up and leave the house, okay? You can't fight her, especially if she throws bricks and things. Will you promise me? If she causes any trouble, you just leave."

He chuckled now. "I didn't know you cared."

She slapped his backside with her free hand. "I didn't say I cared, but I do now have a vested interest in your body."

He started to laugh—loud, husky guffaws that shook his body and interfered with his ability to walk straight. "Oh, Paige, you're priceless." He continued to laugh, in between sloppy, badly placed kisses on her mouth and cheeks, as they meandered crookedly down the deserted street.

***

The house was dark and silent, but they didn't stop to turn the lights on as they cuddled each other and stumbled down the passage to Paige's room. He'd already unclipped her bra by the time they reached the bedroom, and she cursed the lack of central heating as he dragged her jumper, top, and bra over her head, leaving her naked and covered in goose bumps from the waist up. Her nipples stood out pointy and pink, as much from the cold as her arousal.

"Good grief, let's get under the covers. It's so cold in here."

" Important note to self—must get the heating done before winter." Logan gave her a gentle push.

She plonked down on the edge of the bed. Within seconds, she stripped off the remainder of her clothes and jumped under the covers. The sheets were cold and silky on her skin, and she shivered. Logan lunged under the covers and pulled her into his warm embrace.

He hugged her against his solid chest, mindful of his scratches, and rubbed his big, warm hands up and down her arms and over her buttocks. His touch stoked a fiery heat inside and out. When he captured her mouth with his, covering it, plundering it, she met his invasion with enthusiasm, her tongue tangling with his.

With warm hands he cupped her breasts and massaged their softness, teasing her nipples into rosy erectness. After kissing her mouth thoroughly he moved along her neck, flicking his tongue across her earlobe before planting hot kisses over the curve of her shoulder. With a fleeting touch of fire he marked each breast with his mouth then trailed all the way past her rib cage to her abdomen. She entangled her fingers in his hair and moaned as her body sizzled under his kisses.

With clumsy enthusiasm he burrowed under the duvet.

Paige giggled as he continued to mark her with tingling caresses all the way down to her thighs while his fingers lightly tickled her. She parted her legs and still under the duvet, he slid over her leg and settled himself between them. Paige watched the duvet swell and sink with his movements and smiled before she closed her eyes and gave herself up to the growing ache between her legs and the ministrations of her hidden lover.

When he began to explore her outer mound, she drew her knees up a little and opened herself up to him.

With infinite care, he explored her smooth silken outer lips, nibbling, and sucking on each one. Exquisite shooting sensations raced through her. She moaned as he parted her inner lips. The strokes of his tongue were firm and confident as he explored every inch of flesh until he finally settled on her clit.

He licked its tip, sending vibrating waves of arousal rolling over her body. Her clit throbbed as his tongue slid around its base, but when he began to suck, ever so gently, she instinctively lifted her hips to him and whimpered. A groan and a sigh slipped out as the sensation centered on her clit then fanned out through her pussy and outer lips before flooding her abdomen with an aching throb.

His fingers played at the entrance of her pussy—caressing, squeezing and slipping inside just a fraction.

She cried out now, unable to hold back as tremor after tremor shook her body. Her legs moved restlessly as the sensation spread and his fingers thrust into her dripping pussy. He continued to suck on her clit as he rotated his fingers. She squirmed, her whole body quivering and throbbing as it raced towards the brink.

She heaved her hips up against the motion of his fingers and arched her back as she threw her head back in a desperate effort to draw in enough air as her body was pounded by wave after wave of shudders. Her climax consumed her reason as she clenched her pussy down on his fingers in response to a huge wave of erotic energy that engulfed her. As she pushed against it her breathing halted and she crunched her body inward as the molten blast tore through her.

The sensation centered on her pussy for a fraction of a second then it pounded through her. The magnitude of her release stripped her of substance, and she collapsed into the mattress as her strength was swept from her bones. She gasped and laid her head against the pillow, sweat glistening on her skin. A shuddering moan rumbled through her and she lay still, letting the aftershocks flutter across her skin. Her pussy throbbed. It was tight and full.

Logan lightly massaged her by pressing her outer lips together and rubbing his hand over her mound gently dissipating the tension into relaxing relief.

She had barely sighed with satisfaction when she became aware of his more urgent touches.

He was sucking again, tasting her fluids, dipping his tongue into her pussy and sending sparks igniting through her lower body. Then he was moving upwards—licking, kissing and nibbling as he did so. He took her nipple in his mouth and sucked hard while all the time one hand was still playing with her inner lips and stroking her clit.

He captured her mouth and she tasted herself on his lips.

He was lying on top of her, resting between her legs, his weight supported on his hands.

Desperate to have him inside her

Paige slipped her hand down between them and grasped his hard cock. She stroked his shaft a couple of times then guided him to the entrance of her pussy. There was no delay this time as he slid in steadily and firmly until all his cock was buried in her.

She moaned now as his hardness filled her. She could feel his head caressing her cervix. He was gentle. She stared up into his grey eyes, so dark now they were almost black. She lifted her hips slightly in invitation. He smiled and began to thrust. No gentleness now.

Deep, hard thrusts all the way in and almost all the way out, as he stroked her pussy with his whole length.

She lifted her hips to match his rhythm as her body pulsed and vibrated with each plunge of his cock into her body. She hooked her legs around his hips, locking them together in a frantic race to reach the heights. She clutched the bed sheets as he pounded into her, each thrust inflaming her body more, building on the tension of the last one. It was almost unbearable.

Her body shuddered under the force of her climax as it exploded, wrapping itself with tight clutches around his cock, as it penetrated her pulsating flesh. He groaned above her. She cried out as her body was heaved into its release, even as she felt his cock throb rhythmically with its own release.

He sank deep into her and lay still; their bodies vibrated in unison as their climaxes bounced off each other to draw their bodies into a pulsing throbbing embrace. They both gasped and sucked in huge breaths of air as their bodies began to unwind and the explosion of their joint release began to mellow, relaxing muscles and melting bones in complete satiation.

He rolled off her, pulling her with him to encase her in a tight embrace.

"You, my little ghost hunter, are an extraordinary woman."

She snuggled against him. "And you, Logan, are an extraordinary man.

He nuzzled her neck, his hands idly caressing her body. "I think we might have something special."

She covered his slowly moving hands with her own. "I think we might."

They lay together in a cocoon of satiation and warmth. Just before Paige slipped into sleep, she became conscious of Logan's soft snores and even breathing. She was beginning to feel she could trust this man who held her in his sleep. *Maybe… just maybe.*

"Whore! You bed a killer… my killer."

The words screeched into the night quiet. The bed shuddered. The covers were ripped from her body. Clawed fingers dug into her ankle. She was being dragged across the bed.

Paige clutched at the sheet, kicking her free ankle to dislodge the imprisoning hand. "Logan! Save me, Logan."

She hit the floor with a thud.

"Whore, whore. You bed my killer's spawn. How could you." The voice rose to a demented scream.

Paige kicked and fought her motion across the floor. She tried to dig her nails into the carpet, but she couldn't secure a decent hold.

"Paige. Paige." Logan's voice was muffled, distant.

She could hardly hear him through the swirling voices and sensations that surrounded her—clutching hands and muttered threats—thousands of entities all around her, haranguing her, abusing her, and all the time, the ghost yelling threats and abuse.

"Paige, where are you?"

Her vision was blurred, Logan's voice muffled. Paige felt like she was under water, but surrounded by a multitude of unhappy beings.

"You will die, Daughter—your punishment for betrayal."

"He is not a killer, damn you. Let me go. You're dead. Do you hear me, dead. Leave us alone."

The hardness of the floor slammed against her buttocks, the air cleared, the hands and the voices vanished. Logan was there, reaching for her. His hands were cold, his face grey.

"Good grief, Paige, I couldn't reach you. I couldn't touch you. I thought you were dead."

She was gasping for air. Tears trickled down her cheeks.

"She wanted to hurt me. So so angry."

Logan pulled her into his arms and rocked her gently. "You're safe now, Paige. You're safe."

Chapter Six

They both eventually slept, albeit uneasily, after their early morning terror but were still jumpy the next morning. Logan recognized Paige's need to get out of the house and he wished he was joining her on her jaunt to the city library. He wasn't prepared to admit he was scared of his paranormal companion, but he was prepared to admit the feelings of contentment that had embraced him since moving into the house had dimmed somewhat.

But he was not ready to give up his enjoyment of getting his hands dirty in creating something elegant out of dilapidated. He stripped his T-shirt off and, clad in only jeans and steel-capped boots, he set to work pulling up the stained and threadbare carpets in the room they planned to turn into the master bedroom. Even though it was cool, sweat beaded on his bare skin as he heaved and pulled up the carpet and the heavy straw-like underlay. When he caught himself watching over his shoulder for the umpteenth time, he threw down his tools and stomped outside. Chilling laughter rippled through the house behind him.

Furious that he had let her get the better of him, he drank his coffee and returned to work. The door slammed shut behind him the moment he entered the room. He turned. She was just standing there, fully clothed and glaring at him.

"You cannot have her, killer's spawn." She pointed out the window. "Leave my house."

Logan drew himself up to his full height of six foot three and glared back at her. He held the pinch bar he had been using to remove the tacks tightly in his hands. Although what he thought he could achieve with his weapon against a ghost, he didn't know.

The specter glided towards him and eerie laugh rippled around the space—a tinkling melodic sound with an icy edge.

He waited and watched.

She glided closer. "You cannot have her—I will not let you tarnish my daughter. I shall milk you dry of desire. Milk you dry of life itself unless you leave my house and my daughter."

"No, damn you. I will not leave. You cannot stop me from loving Paige and she is not your daughter."

He felt the chill as the specter touched his body.

She breathed chilled mist into his face. He coughed once then he reached for her, pulled her closer, even as she massaged his cock through his jeans.

He ached already with the desire to possess her—to meld his flesh with her hot wet pussy. And yet he cringed away from the desire, repulsed by her. All he wanted was Paige. The hot length of his penis throbbed in its confined space and with hurried clumsiness, he undid his fly and dragged his jeans and underwear down his thighs. His prominent erection sprang out, hard and throbbing.

With misty hands she caressed it. He moaned as the ache spread through his body. He resented his body's betrayal and tried to shake off the raging desire that flounced through him.

She laughed again.

The hard edge of the sound penetrated the fog of sexual possession. He tried to pull away fighting the fog of lust that held him.

He was in trouble. Terror surged through him when he couldn't pull away. His whole body was tormented with the need to sink his ramrod stiff shaft into her pussy. So much so, he trembled and struggled to remain upright.

The semi translucent form sank to her knees before him and took his whole length into her mouth. She sucked hard on the head then slid her lips down the shaft. Well shaped hands cupped his balls and squeezed, hard.

He groaned. The sensation hovered between pleasure and pain.

She slid up and down his shaft. He stood there powerless to stop her or his response. His hips began to thrust. She sucked then, sucked and sucked until his climax charged through his body, up his shaft and burst into thick cum in her mouth.

His knees weakened. Even as his orgasm still pulsed through him he fell backward. He landed with a thud on the roll of carpet. He looked up at her. "Get away from me."

She stood over him. "You cannot resist me. I will suck you dry. There will be nothing left to sully my daughter with. Go now, while you can."

He lay there, his jeans and trunks tangled around his ankles, the rest of his body naked and exposed. His cock ached. It still stood out hard. He felt as if he hadn't come at all. He reached down and rubbed his turgid flesh and squeezed his balls, trying to ease the discomfort.

She laughed. "There will be no comfort for you, killer's spawn."

In a tiny corner of his mind, he knew he was in danger, but all he wanted to do was pull her down beside him and sink his shaft into her.

"You're mine. There is nothing left to sully my daughter."

"She's not your daughter. You're dead. You have been dead for years."

"No, no, no! You lie! Be gone."

The carpet shuddered beneath him, roiling and humping. It rose above him and dropped with suffocating weight. Then it twisted and turned and wound itself around him. He struggled as the realization he was in more danger than just being unfaithful to Paige. He was in real danger of losing his life. His fear shattered her spell, and galvanized him into action. Too late. He was being bound tightly in the dank dusty one hundred year old carpet.

He struggled to breathe as the dust and grit filled his nose, eyes, and mouth. He could not loosen his arms where they were pinned at his sides. Then the carpet stilled. He lay bound, naked, and with little air to drag into his lungs. He lay still and tried to ease his breathing. Logically, he didn't think he would be suffocated because carpet was a woven fabric, but the desire to struggle, kick, and scream bounced around his mind. He forced himself to stay still. He could hear her laughter from his tomb. The door slammed. Silence and guilt engulfed him.

***

Paige was excited by her discoveries at the city library and had a folder full of photocopies; photos, birth and death certificates, ship's passenger lists, and logs. Lots of pieces of the jigsaw that would hopefully, in conjunction with Sarah's diaries, provide the answers to their ghost's anguish and hostility towards Logan. She couldn't wait to show him.

The house was silent and deserted when she arrived home. His car was there so she assumed he was in the house or garden. She made coffee and spread her materials out on the table. Still he hadn't appeared, so taking her coffee with her, she wandered through the rooms.

"Logan, are you here?" She shouted several times, but her voice just echoed back to her from the empty rooms. It wasn't until she reached the front room that she began to really feel uneasy. His tools were all over the place. "Logan?"

She stepped over the large roll of carpet and underlay and looked out of the window. She turned back to the room. She could almost smell him—that tangy scent of his toiletries mixed with his own unique male scent. It was subtle, almost masked by the stale dusty smell of the carpet. *Where was he?*

She pulled out her mobile and dialed his number. She heard his phone ring, faint, but near, the thudding rhythms of AC/DC's heavy metal anthem, "T.N.T." She moved toward it. It was coming from inside the roll of carpet. She disconnected, shoved her phone in her pocket, and pounced on the old floor covering. It was heavy and awkward as she tried to unroll it. Dust rose and clogged her throat as she thrashed with the tangled twelve-foot cylinder of woven fabric. She tugged and pulled until she finally managed to roll it one turn, then another. Sweat poured down her face and trickled between her breasts.

"Come on. Move," she screamed at it as she grunted and gasped. She rolled it again, moving up and down the length.

"Logan, can you hear me. Logan!" There was no reply. She felt sick. Her stomach churned and her chest constricted. She struggled to breathe through exertion and fear.

"Logan!" She screamed his name as finally the last coil unraveled to reveal her unconscious lover. He was pale, his skin was dry to touch, and his breathing barely perceptible.

She patted his face. "Logan, can you hear me? Open your eyes."

He groaned and turned his head away from her hand.

She leapt up, ran to the kitchen, and came back with a bottle of chilled water and a cloth. She wiped his face with the wet material.

He moaned.

As she splashed more water on his face and chest, she realized for the first time he was as good as naked with his jeans and boxer briefs bunched around his ankles. She could smell the sex on him. A rush of jealousy poured through her. It was tinged with a sense of betrayal. A sense of betrayal she knew was misplaced.

He opened his eyes, and tried to focus on her face. "Paige, I'm sorry. I couldn't stop her...couldn't resist..."

She lifted his head and helped him sip the cool water.

"Paige?"

She heard the desperation in his voice. "It's okay, Logan. Let's get you in the shower and cool you down." She helped him into a sitting position.

He sipped more water as she tugged his clothes and boots off.

Entirely naked now, she pulled him to his feet and tucked an arm around his waist as he hugged her shoulders to support himself. With shuffling steps, they made the excruciatingly painful journey to the bathroom.

Logan sat on the edge of the bath while Paige adjusted the water and grabbed the plastic linen basket, emptied the clothes on the floor, and turned it upside down. She placed it in the shower alcove, and ignoring the cool water soaking her. It was awkqard in the enclosed space but with a lot of maneuvering she sat Logan on it. As she ripped her soggy tee and shorts off, Logan sat on the makeshift chair, his hands on his thighs, his head hanging down, letting the water pour over his head.

He looked up as she stepped back into the alcove. His face was full of anguish. "I'm sorry…"

"Shhh." She shampooed his hair and began on his body to wash away the grit and smell of the old carpet. It was erotic, sliding her hands over his firm, smooth skin and she almost immediately felt her pussy tingle with awareness. Logan just sat there, unmoving. She moved down to caress his back, abdomen, and thighs. Then she moved to his cock, determined to wash away the evidence of his sexual encounter with the ghost.

She massaged his balls and slid her hand up and down his cock. Logan moaned softly at her gentle strokes, but his cock remained flaccid. She slid her hand under him and stroked. Even with the lack of response she leaned down to kiss him.

He immediately responded with a demanding pressure that almost begged her to elicit a response from his body. His hands reached up and stroked her streaming body, then slipped between her legs. His fingers explored her lips and dipped into her pussy. She arched back and parted her legs to give him access but his hands dropped away.

She opened her eyes and realized his cock lay still and soft over the mound of his balls. She was suddenly cold in the cool water and without comment, turned the water off and reached for a towel. She handed a second one to Logan, noticing his face was a sickly grey as he stared down at himself like he had never seen his crown jewels before.

"Logan?"

He looked up at her now. "She said she would take away my desire, to stop me making love to you. I so want you, Paige but…"

"Stand, Logan. What you need is more water to rehydrate you, and rest. Your body is traumatized by being in the carpet—that's all. I do not, for a moment, believe a ghost can prevent you from getting it up."

Logan followed her instructions, getting into her bed, drinking the water she thrust at him then eating the soup she heated for them. He looked better. The color had returned to his face, and his body was back to normal temperature. He lay in the bed and watched her pack up their bowls before she slipped off her bathrobe.

She rested her head on his shoulder and listened to his heart beating under her ear. With the residue of desire still simmering between her legs, she toyed with the idea of trying to arouse him, but immediately discarded it. He didn't need another failure tonight to reinforce the uneasiness he already felt. He needed rest far more than sex, so she snuggled close to him and laid her arm over his hips, just below his wounds.

She told him about her finds in the library, and how her drawing was almost a replica of an old photograph she had found of Annie Dunsford on her wedding day. She also revealed that Annie's death certificate listed her as 'lost at sea'.

"So if it's not Annie, who is it?"

"I think it is Annie. I don't think she ever got on that boat. It was probably just a story concocted to explain her disappearance. Gosh, there is so much to think about."

"Including staying alive."

She kissed him gently on the cheek. "Yes, including staying alive. I am not going to leave you alone in this house again. It's too dangerous. Do you want to forfeit the inheritance? I mean, I don't want to, but I would understand if you've had enough of the haunting."

"The more she tries to get rid of me, the more determined I am to stay, and damn her, she's dead. If it is Annie, she's been dead almost one hundred and fifty years. This is our time. She's had hers."

"Are you sure?"

He kissed her hard on the mouth. "Yes, I'm sure."

***

A spine-chilling cat's battle screech ripped her from sleep. She opened her eyes to find the room was lit with an eerie glow. Immediately, she rolled over and found Logan lying on his back. His eyes were open, but unblinking, as he stared ahead while his mouth moved as if he was kissing someone. Off to his side, level with his chest, she could see the translucent shape of the ghost she now thought of as Annie. She was naked. Her hands were caressing his abdomen while she kissed him, covering his mouth completely with her own questing lips. His hand was moving and Paige could see he was stroking between her legs. His eyes were open, but he did not respond to Paige when she touched his arm.

Anger fired through her as she sat up, climbed to her knees, and glared at the apparition. "Go, Annie. Leave him be. He is not for the likes of you."

The ghost stared back at her, for a long moment then began to laugh. "He's not for the likes of you either, Daughter. He's a killer's get. Go now... away from this evil."

Paige reached out to stay the apparition's hand as it reached for Logan's cock, which was standing upright, hard and throbbing. She felt the chill as her hand passed through the vision.

The ghost laughed again. "You can't stop me," she screeched. "I hold him."

Paige ignored her, and made a grab for Logan's cock. She enclosed its hot length in her hands, even as Annie reached for it. Despite the chill surrounding her hands, Paige realized that Annie could not penetrate through her living flesh.

Annie glared at her. "He is mine," the specter muttered, before she turned away and began to kiss Logan again.

Paige could see him passionately smothering Annie's mouth. One hand cupped her large breast and caressed her prominent erect nipple, while his other was buried between her legs. From the movement, it was obvious he was caressing her pussy and clit.

Burning rage washed over Paige, driven by fierce jealousy and un-bridled fear—a jealousy and a fear that gave her the strength and agility to jump over Logan so she straddled his hips with his cock standing up in front of her pubic mound. She felt a force push and almost unseat her. She pushed back with no effect.

Annie laughed again from where she was now sitting astride Lo-gan's chest facing Paige. Paige could see Logan's hands caressing be-tween her legs and dipping into her pussy. She wanted to knock his hands away with a fury that was as strong as if her lover's partner was a flesh and blood woman.

"You can't stop me. See. He wants me. Not you. Desire makes a man hard. He had no desire for you tonight," Annie's ghost boasted.

"Of course not. No man would after he had been abused and almost suffocated by you. Whatever is happening to him now is not real. Like you, Annie—just an apparition..."

Annie reached up to push her away. "Ah, but one he enjoys. One you cannot compete with. See he is going soft even as you hold him."

Acutely aware that Logan's cock was losing some of its turgid hardness and tried not to panic as she wondered if it was lack of desire for her or him consciously fighting Annie.

"Logan, wake up. Open your eyes."

Logan stirred and moaned. Paige pumped his cock with some energy. It wavered in her hands.

She pumped harder. "Wake up. It's Paige."

He threw his head from side to side and moaned.

Annie tried to kiss him again, but he turned his head away. The ghost glared at Paige, and Paige knew then that she was in some way penetrating Annie's hold on Logan's mind and body.

"Logan, it's Paige. I'm about to fuck you. I'm going to sit on your cock."

She lifted herself, and with some maneuvering, she mounted his cock and let it slide into her. She wasn't as wet as she would have liked, but the weight of her downward movement pushed his cock deep into her pussy. It filled her, rubbing slightly abrasively on the delicate inner walls. As she settled down hard on his erection, she reached down and began to stoke her own clit, softly at first then harder, more urgently. Her body responded to the stimulation and her pussy began to tingle around the hard cock shoved inside. She clenched and unclenched her pussy muscles on his cock.

He groaned.

"Logan, it's me, Paige. Your cock is buried deep in my pussy. She can't touch it."

Annie rose up over Paige as she sat impaled on Logan's hard cock and reached out with clawed hands to grab Paige's breasts. Paige sat still and stared Annie down, daring her to continue the assault on Logan.

Finally, the ghost wailed and retreated. For a while, the specter circled them.

Paige shivered. She knew if the ghost attacked, there would be little she could do to protect them, as Logan lay there, his cock buried deep in her body.Without taking her eyes of the apparition hovering inches away, Paige lifted herself a fraction then pushed downwards, and again.

"Logan, start thrusting if you're aware it's me. We can beat her."

She felt the slightest of movements from him, and she immediately met it with one of her own.

Logan moaned. The apparition that wanted to fuck him so badly, screeched—once, twice, three times, before she melted into the darkness.

Paige rose and pushed downwards and was met by a strong upward thrust from Logan's hips. They moved in unison. Paige continued to rub her clit and the combination of his thrusting and her stroking brought on a rush of sensation. It spread in tingling waves over her body then centered on her pussy. She moved faster and pushed down harder until she felt Logan match her rhythm. His hands came up now and grasped her hips as their rhythm increased.

Logan stared up at Paige.

She saw recognition in his eyes. She almost cried with relief. He knew who he was fucking.

He watched her masturbating herself. His breath came in fast, short gasps. Then the tension exploded and flooded her body with blasts of incredible heat. Paige cried out and moved faster on his cock while he met each of her downward pushes. As her climax eased, his began ripple after ripple undulated along his cock from the base to the head. With each pulse, his hot cum squirt against her sensitive flesh. She squeezed her pussy muscles with each throb, making Logan groan with intensity before he buried himself deep inside her. For a long moment, they were motionless with only the rasp of their breathing breaking the silence. Paige collapsed onto his chest, his hard cock still inside her.

He wrapped his arms around her and nuzzled her neck.

"Oh my God, Paige. You saved me from a fate worse than death."

She smiled and kissed his damp skin. One to her, zero to the ghost. They lay for a long time, still joined, and it wasn't until Paige felt his flaccid cock eventually slide out of her pussy, did she move to lower herself to his side.

He held her tightly against his body, whispering his thanks over and over in her ear until finally he lay back and slept.

She watched the darkness, and listened, for a long time, but there was no sign of Annie's return. Finally, physical and emotional exhaustion took its toll, and she also slept.

The thump of AC/DC's heavy metal music dragged them both from sleep. Logan sounded groggy during the long call, but it seemed as if the person on the other end had the most to say.

Logan hung up and rolled out of bed.

"Up, my love. We are having visitors in about an hour." He took her hands in his and pulled her to her knees. He embraced her in a brief, hard hug, followed by a lingering kiss. "My woman, my ghost slayer. Where would I be without you? Your loving dragged me from the pit of the apparition's seduction."

She kissed him back. "So, who are our visitors?"

"The detective who came to exhume the skeleton and his niece. Apparently, she has to do a field assignment for her Masters in Criminology and wants to use our skeleton. It's a rare opportunity apparently. She plans to identify the skeleton by examining the bones, measuring them, and stuff—facial reconstruction, that sort of thing, and DNA, if possible."

"Oh wow. That will be interesting," Paige said.

"It will, and even better, if it can lay the bitch to rest. I've had about as much as I can cope with."

She kissed him again. "Well, at least now I know how to make her back off—make love to you."

He laughed now. "That you can do any time, my love."

She reached out and caressed his cock. It immediately began to stiffen.

"But not right now." He chuckled and swung his hips and his cock away from her seeking hands. "Much as the thought is appealing, time is short."

Just over an hour later, Detective Moody and his niece, Christine, arrived. She was a serious and very organized young woman. Detective Moody firstly informed them that a preliminary study of the skeleton had revealed it was female, at least one hundred years old, and also showed evidence of trauma to the skull that could indicate a murder. It seemed as if the skull had been smashed by a blunt instrument. The dead woman had also been pregnant with a male child—about four months on.

Christine explained what she wanted to achieve and how she would do it. They took a tour of the house and the burial site, and they talked about the possible haunting of the house. When her uncle left, they adjourned to the kitchen for coffee and together pored over the materials Paige had found at the library. Christine asked how they were both related to Annie. Paige said she was a direct descendent, but Logan admitted he was not quite sure. She took DNA samples from them both, although she wasn't sure she could match it to the skeleton because of age.

When Paige agreed, Christine gathered up all the documentation on a promise to photocopy it and return it the next day.

Paige didn't allow her to take the diaries, but said she would read them herself and take notes on relevant items. Christine planned to make a reconstruction of the face using a model of the skull and doing tests on the bones and other revealing markers like teeth and skeletal dimensions. She said it would be challenging because of the age of the skeleton but was pleased because it would look good on her report.

Paige was quite excited as they waved Christine off and was eager to begin her contribution to the project.

Logan laughed as they walked back to the house.

"Sounds like you are making it your personal project to find out who she is."

She stopped and stood on tip toes, so she could reach his mouth. She kissed him hard, demanding he capitulate to her ruthless exploration. He tightened his grip on her waist, pulled her up to him, and promptly devoured her mouth until he had her gasping for breath and more than a little turned on.

"Logan Dunsford–Hamilton, you are a very sexy, demanding man. Why would I not want to make it my personal business to identify the ghost and banish her. I do not like to share, and you are most definitely mine. What say we bring the rest of those boxes from the attic so I can really get to work?"

It didn't take long to pull down the stairs and climb into the attic. There were three boxes containing journals of varying age and condition. Logan went down the stairs halfway and Paige handed him the boxes. He placed them on the passage floor and returned to the attic.

He looked around. "There's a lot to explore up here. I suspect we should sift through it all before they come to re-roof. Much of it will probably end up in the skip, but there might be some historically valuable items." He stood balanced on the top step.

"Die, killer. Die."

Paige saw the ghost out of the corner of her vision. She swept forward, her hands outstretched.

"Logan, watch out."

It was too late. Ghostly hands connected with Paige's back. The force thrust her toward Logan. She resisted the momentum. Her shoes dragged in the dust. "I can't stop her. Move Logan, move. Her hands touched Logan's chest unbalancing him.

He clutched at the rope handrails and managed to slow his tumble to an inelegant slide until he hit the floor with a thud. "Damn, damn, damn."

Paige stood frozen. She peered down at Logan lying on the floor. "I didn't mean to push you. I didn't mean to."

Logan stared up at her, his expression grim. "Watch out, Paige she's right behind you."

Paige swung around and glared at the quietly approaching apparition. She pointed her finger at the specter. "Don't touch me. Go from here. You've done enough damage, ghost."

The ghost kept approaching, shaking her head in denial. "Not enough, Daughter, for the killer remains. You abandoned me. You let him dig me up. This house will never be yours."

The ghost rushed at her and even as Paige tried to brace herself on the door frame, she was falling. She clutched to the rope rails and scrabbled for a foothold. Then she landed in a pair of strong arms trembling from the shock of her fall. Deep grief came surging back with further memories of the past that had burst the closed door in her mind open.

She pushed out of Logan's arms. "Don't touch me. I'm evil. I've tried to kill you before, Logan. I did it..."

He reached for her.

She stumbled out of his reach.

"Paige, it's all right. Calm down."

Huge sobs wrenched at her throat, tears poured down her face. "Don't try to soothe me. I am to blame for it all. I did it—they told me I was evil, a budding psychopath, a killer. My parents had me locked up—for treatment..."

"Paige, stop."

She shook her head. "No. I remember now. I blamed you, for lying about who hurt you, for making my father so ashamed he left us, but it was me. Always, it was me. He left when Mum took me out of that place—she refused to accept their diagnosis because she loved me. She believed me about the ghost—she and Sarah were the only ones who believed me." She looked up at Logan. "How can you bear to touch me, turn your back on me, sleep with me? She used me to try and kill you—then and now."

Logan shook his head and stepped forward. "You were a baby, Paige, just a baby. It wasn't really you. It was that bloody ghost. She made you."

It was her turn to shake her head. "But you can't stay here. She can make me do things—bad things. Like now. Like before."

"No," he said quietly, as he stepped forward and pulled her into his arms.

She held herself stiffly against him. She no longer knew how to react. He stroked her hair and began to kiss her face. She pulled back, but he wouldn't let her go.

"How can you ever trust me?" How... we have no future. I knew... I knew from the beginning it was dangerous to be in the house with you. I knew somehow."

"Shhh, now." Logan hugged her. "What say we go out for the afternoon and grab some dinner? We both need a break from the evil and oppression of this damn house and I want some time to spend with you—without having to fight off ghosts, apparitions or any other ethereal specters."

"But this changes everything."

"No, it doesn't. Now, do you want to get away from here?"

She surrendered to his easy words of comfort, even though inside the turmoil rampaged. "Mmmm, sounds wonderful. What say we go to Victor Harbor? It's cold but sunny, and a walk along the beach should clear our heads."

***

The beach was almost deserted. Seaweed rolled up the sand, pushed by the wind and sea. Small breakers crashed on the water's edge, sending white foam bouncing in the air and scurrying up the beach. The cold, crisp air smelled strongly of seaweed and salt. Paige felt warm and protected, as they ambled together along the beach. Logan held her close against his body, pausing every few paces to kiss her with infinite tenderness. At the causeway, they stood and stared out to sea.

"What are we going to do with all this? Do you want to leave the house?"

"No."

"I'm worried about your safety, from me and her. She seems very determined to harm you—what with the bricks, the carpet and trying to suck your life force out."

"I am worried about her too, but not enough to walk away. In fact, I'm determined to beat her."

"I wonder why she hates you so much?"

Logan shrugged. "Who knows? Maybe those diaries might have a clue or two."

"Maybe. I am going to do a timeline as well. Sarah has drawn up a family tree. It's a bit rough but has lots of names and dates."

"Well, Christine might also come up with something interesting."

"She might, but for now, how about we come up with some dinner. I'm starving. It must be all the fresh sea air."

After they ordered, Logan stared directly into her eyes.

"I want you to promise me to never, ever give a thought to what happened when we were kids. Whatever happened was not your fault. You were a baby and forced by that entity to do bad things. Now promise, Paige."

She stared at him for a long moment, unsure what to say. "I am not sure I can. I can never forget my father's judgment of me, his fury. Having me locked up and leaving us when my mother released me. Could they have all been so wrong, Logan?"

"Yes, they were wrong. Case closed."

Again she shook her head. "Can you really trust me unconditionally, after what I did today? I pushed you."

"No the ghost pushed you into me and I fell."

"Yes but..."

"No buts. And I have a confession to make. I know you were not responsible for the shelf falling in the shed. I knew, because I saw you swinging on the clothes hoist just before the shelf started to fall. I knew I wasn't supposed to be in there. I didn't want a beating from my father, so I lied. I didn't realize it would lead to so much trouble for you, because I blamed you for all the times I was naughty or clumsy—anything to get out of a strapping from my Dad. It was not just the ones you were responsible for. I'm sorry, Paige. Can you trust me?"

Paige started to laugh then.

"We were such a pair of wallies. I hated you blaming me all the time and I was really angry with you in the attic, but I wouldn't have pushed you, unless she made me."

"I never thought your father would be so ruthless towards you."

Paige shrugged then. "Maybe he wasn't, but just looking for a way out. He didn't always treat Mum with respect. Who knows?"

"Pretty gutless, I think. Anyway, I actually consider myself to be a very lucky man to have such a beautiful, feisty woman on my side." He reached out and picked up her hand, his large fingers caressing the palm as he cupped it. "My ghost slayer."

Paige smiled. "I thought you were very enamored with your dream lover. You said she was very beautiful."

"Yes. She looks like you—sort of. But being with you, is different. The incidents with her were physically incredible, but emotionally empty. I didn't realize it until I made love to you for the first time. What we shared was mind blowing, but also heart and soul nurturing."

"You could tell the difference?"

His grim expression hardened his features for a moment. "When you were fighting her last night for possession of my body, I could tell when you touched me and when... when I slipped inside you. It was like a warm embrace... I can only suppose that it comes with loving the woman you love."

"Love, Logan?"

He smiled again. "Yes, love, Paige. I never thought I would say that to another woman, but it is the only word that describes how I feel about you. I think I might have loved you since we were kids." He picked up her other hand. "I'm not certain I am ready just yet to walk up the aisle or anything like that, but I feel deeply about you and spending time with you is important to me. I want to explore what there is between us—what there could be—to build the trust between us. I would like to think we have enough to begin healing the wounds of betrayal and broken trust we both have."

She looked at him. The obvious desire and love in his eyes shadowed the orbs. A multitude of thoughts raged through her mind. There was so much between them and she wondered if two people with such a complicated history could move past it. Could two broken people learn to trust again—to heal each other? They'd come a long way in a short time as they both struggled with the challenges that had come with Sarah Hamilton's bizarre bequest, and their own insecurities brought to the fore by their situation. Was there enough left in each of them to build something new? She wasn't sure, but suddenly she hoped there was. With a tentative smiled and squeezed his hands. "I too, would like to think we can build something of our own."

He lifted her hand and kissed the tips of her fingers.

***

As they pulled into the drive, Logan felt the tension tighten in his chest. He would really love to back out onto the road and leave the house forever, but he was determined not to give into this paranormal phenomenon that had begun to make his life a misery. He had also done something tonight he had sworn he would never do again; tell a woman he loved her. He had been so passionately besotted with his ex-wife and so gutted by her unfaithfulness, he swore never to give his heart again. Tonight he had, and it scared him. Paige was beautiful, intelligent, funny, determined, and feisty. The whole package had him bewitched from the first meeting in the lawyer's office that had surprisingly revived his childhood connection with Paige.

Now, as she sat beside him in the darkness of the car, he knew he had not made a mistake—he did love her, he did want her. All they had to do was get past this damn revengeful ghost, who was not only determined to keep them apart, but was trying her hardest to remove him from the house, either by scaring him badly enough or outright killing him. He was still uneasy about the ghost's influence on Paige—the influence that, so many years ago, had almost cost him his life. He sensed her reluctance, like his, to go into the house. He turned and found she was watching him.

"Are you sure you want to do this?"

Logan nodded. "I am not sure I want to, but I am going to. I will not be defeated by a spook."

She laughed now. "Not even such a beautiful one."

"No, not even such a beautiful one. She just has to learn beauty alone just doesn't do it. I need a live woman with a pulse, breath, warmth, personality, and a hot, wet pussy."

"Well then, let's get on with it." She opened the door, climbed out of the car, and started walking towards the dark and silent house.

He hurried after her, determined the woman he loved would not have to face the ghost's wrath alone.

Logan was exhausted as he slipped under the duvet and gathered her soft, warm body against his. He snuggled down and breathed in her scent—warm woman, tangy sea air, and a delicate lingering of her flowery perfume. She snuggled close. All he wanted to do tonight was hold her. He didn't have the energy to make love to her with the enthusiasm she deserved, and he was grateful that she seemed to sense how he felt and made no move to arouse him. He kissed her neck and nuzzled her ear. "I want to just hold you all night."

"Mmmmm."

They lay in silence. Logan felt his cock become semi-hard from her body pressing against him, but he ignored it. Tonight was about love and closeness, not about sex. He listened to her steady breathing as he inhaled her scent. His heart beat faster as tender emotions washed over him, and he knew it wouldn't take much for him to make a commitment to this woman. At last he relaxed and drifted into sleep.

***

It was daylight when he opened his eyes. The air was cool on his face and Paige was still asleep, spooned against him. Her hair was tousled, her full lips pouting, and long, dark lashes brushed her cheeks. He moaned softly. He so wanted her. His cock was hard, so hard with need, and he always loved a morning session. He was reluctant to wake her, but he wanted her so badly.

He cupped her breasts with his hands and gently stroked the soft skin with his thumb. His fingers teased her nipples into erect rosy little nubs before he slid his hand down over her mound and dipped his fingers into the moist layers of flesh that protected the entrance to her pussy. He caressed her lips, then with tender strokes, massaged her clit.

Responding to his attention Paige stirred now, stretching contentedly, as a tiny moan escaped from her lips. She didn't open her eyes or give him any indication she was awake.

With the hand under her, he continued to caress her clit. With the other hand, he stroked her butt cheeks then slid his hand between them, moving with exaggerated slowness down the crack and between her legs. He felt the moisture as he slid his fingers up between her lips and into her pussy.

A soft moan eased out of her and she stirred her body slightly to give him access.

He slid two fingers in and out of her pussy in simultaneous rhythm to his strokes on her clit, making her moan again. He lifted his cock and placed it at the bottom of her buttocks with just the head inserted between her legs.

She lifted her top leg ever so slightly and pressed back against him, allowing his cock to slide between her thighs until he felt the head sinking into her wetness. He lifted his hips a little and he felt his head just ease into her pussy. She whimpered now and pressed harder back against him. In the same movement he lifted her top leg and guided his throbbing cock right into her and once fully imbedded inside her, he moved in and out with long, slow strokes.

Her eyes were still shut, but tiny moans and whimpers slipped out between her slightly parted lips. He increased the pace of his movement inside her a little harder and faster, and now he felt her bum move to match his rhythm. His finger stroked her clit in time with his thrusts, alternating between hard and fast and deep and slow. He felt the tremor begin in her legs and he could see her hands gripping the sheet in a tight fist. She pushed back to meet his upward pushes as the tremor became a shudder. She cried out. He sank in deep and fast now, matching his rhythm with his strokes on her clit. He felt her pussy clench and her clit stiffen.

She groaned and hunched down. Her breathing halted and she grunted. He continued to impale her body with his own. He was so close to exploding. He felt her whole body hunch as her climax ripped through her. God, he loved that feeling. Hot fluid squirted out against his cock and ran down his balls. He couldn't hold it any longer and with two hard, deep thrusts, he exploded. Once, twice, three times he felt his cock pump out hot cum. She squeezed his cock each time making the sensation almost beyond bearing. The room spun as his climax charged through his body and he trembled from top to toe. He struggled to breathe. Sweat poured off his body, and all he could do then was lay still, his cock still enclosed in her hot and soaking pussy.

"Mmmmm. Such a divine way to wake up."

He kissed her neck with butterfly soft kisses. She murmured appreciation, but made no attempt to move and Logan was happy with that. He was content to just lie there and hold her in his arms, with his cock wrapped up to the hilt in her. He had slipped deliciously in and out of sleep for about half an hour when the wails began. Spine tingling wails choked down to grunted sobs. Paige started in his arms and his cock slipped right out of her pussy. The movement sparked a slight hardening of his flesh, but the next wail squelched his cock back into floppy softness.

Chapter Seven

"Good grief, what it that terrible noise?"

"I think it is our resident apparition, although to the uninitiated, it sounds like a cross between an out-of-control chainsaw and a tractor that needs a tune up," he replied with a chuckle.

Paige climbed out of bed. She pulled on his T-shirt and padded cautiously towards the bedroom door. She opened it a fraction and peered out. He sat up and swung his legs over the side of the bed. He pulled on his trunks and went to stand beside her. He peered over her shoulder. Nothing moved in the passage but the wails continued. He pressed up against Paige's buttocks. They were warm and soft.

He leaned down and placed a light kiss on her shoulder, as his cock responded to the contact. "What say we go back to bed?"

She looked up at him at the same time as she reached between them and gave his cock a soft squeeze.

Heat shot through his cock and his balls tightened.

"That noise is not very conducive to the correct mood, lover boy. We should find out what the hell is going on."

He leaned closer. "I know, my love. It's just that I can't get enough of you."

"Me either, but..." She took his hand and pulled him through the doorway.

Side by side they walked silently down the passage. The noise seemed to be coming from behind the plastic sheeting Tony had put up. Paige lifted it aside. There she was, kneeling by the hole in the ground from where they'd removed the skeleton. She was dressed in a long skirt, high necked blouse, and had an apron covering her front. She was tearing her hair from her head as she stared down at the hole in the ground. Cat was sitting beside her, washing himself. Logan felt vulnerable with only his boxer briefs to protect his body from her attentions. He held back a little as Paige took several cautious steps toward the distressed apparition.

"Annie?"

The ghost turned. She had tears on her face even as she glared at them, her face a distorted mask of hatred and accusation. "Desecrated! You, my daughter, and the killer's spawn... you have desecrated my last resting place. Desecrated! Haven't I paid enough—been punished enough?"

"Annie, we will have you interred in consecrated ground. Soon, I promise."

The apparition leapt to her feet and glided towards Paige, her hands curled into claws that reached out to attack. Logan wanted to flee, but when Paige stood her ground, he stood solid behind her. They would face this together.

"Annie, stop!" Paige shouted her order and put her hand up to stop the ghost's advance.

The specter stopped on Paige's shout, but Logan could see it trembling with some sort of emotion. Rage? Perhaps, even fear or anguish and he felt a sudden unexpected rush of sympathy for the ghost, and the woman she had been. She had obviously been badly treated and her spirit was afraid of what was happening in the world of the living.

"How dare you let him dig me up? I have been violated. Desecrated. Cursed to forever wander the earth. No peace. Never to rest."

"Annie, digging you up was an accident. He didn't mean anything by it."

The specter began to laugh, a shrill, bitter, shrieking gurgle. "The killer's spawn didn't mean anything—no, he just wants me gone. To protect my killer."

"Annie, he is at least five generations on from whoever killed you. Do not punish him. He is helping me solve your murder."

"Hah! He won't like the answer. He won't. He won't," she screeched as she faded.

When she was gone, the room felt somehow empty. It was as if the ghost had a physical space. Logan slipped his arms around Paige's waist and hugged her.

"My love, my little ghost slayer—come back to bed."

At that moment the phone rang, filling the sunlit space with AC/DC's "T.N.T."

"Damn," he muttered as he answered the call.

It was the plumber to say he would be there in half an hour. He had barely disconnected and it rang again. It was the police this time, giving them permission to continue with the work on the kitchen. They'd finished with the gravesite. He slipped his phone back in the band of his boxer briefs. He pouted childishly at Paige.

"Damn."

She laughed at his mock sulk.

He watched as her face lit up, her eyes sparkled, and her cheeks colored to a soft rose hue. God, she was so beautiful, so sexy. His cock stirred.

She poked her tongue out just a little between her full lips. "Soon. The anticipation will be good for you. Now if you're going to be ready for the plumber, you better take the first shower. I will make coffee and I think we have some muffins in the fridge."

"Never mind the breakfast. Come join me in the shower?" He reached for her, but she skipped away and pointed towards the bathroom.

"Off you go—alone, Logan Dunsford-Hamilton, but leave the door open."

"What? You want to perv?"

Her smile faded now. "I do like to perv, but no. I want the door open in case Annie tries something. She's pretty upset."

Logan felt a chill rush over him. He didn't like the way the ghost controlled him. The way she held him in some sort of trance that he was unable to fight free of.

"Okay. I won't be long."

The house seemed sort of empty and sad today, and Paige wondered if Annie had left. She wandered out when she heard the digger start, concerned that Annie would try one of her nasty tricks, but all was quiet. Back inside on a large sheet of paper, she drew a rough timeline using the dates she had. Then she began dipping into the diaries of Annie and her older daughter, Elizabeth, on relevant dates. Both diaries stopped abruptly, Annie's in 1860, with a half-finished entry on May sixteenth and Elizabeth's finished just over six months later in 1861.

Paige was horrified at Annie's last entry.

He has a son by the whore, Gwen Sealey, and he intends to bring that child to me to raise. I do not want it—as I am sure his mother does not want to lose him. I already carry another of his, maybe a boy this time. The callousness of the man I married stultifies my mind...

Elizabeth's entry about her mother's disappearance was short.

They say Mama ran away, because she wanted to go back to England. Father says she didn't love us. But I don't believe him. On the night Mama disappeared, someone came to the house. When Father returned home five days later, I saw Father and a woman doing something in the kitchen. They were burying something. The next morning, the kitchen had a new floor and we had a new mother. I think they killed Mama and I told them so. I was severely punished by my new mother.

The following entries got briefer. Elizabeth complained that she constantly felt ill. In the last entry, she accused her stepmother of poisoning her to stop her talking to her godfather, Lord Forbes, when he came for her birthday. The younger daughter, Margaret, then took up where her sister had left off. She also lived in constant fear of dying at her stepmother's hand.

Paige got more and more excited as bits and pieces started to fill in the jigsaw. She could hardly contain herself from dragging Logan into the house and explaining to him what she had found.

She still didn't quite know where Logan fit into the puzzle though. She knew that Sarah's older sister, Annabelle, was her great-grandmother, but she was struggling to put Logan's prior generations in place. There seemed to be a piece missing. She pulled out Sarah's diary from her teenage years and another small book fell from inside. It was a journal by someone called Ada—Ada Dunsford. She put it aside and began to read Sarah's thin, spidery hand as she recorded every significant event in her long life. As she reached one of Sarah's references to her beloved brother, she grabbed the discarded diary—Ada

Dunsford's diary. It was filled with pages and pages of her love affair and the illegitimate child she carried after her lover died in the war. Her lover was none other than Thomas Hamilton, Sarah's brother.

She started when Logan touched her on the shoulder. "Interesting, my love?"

"Very. Actually, fascinating. I even know where you fit into the family tree and why Sarah split the inheritance between us."

"Really." He slipped into the chair beside her and laid his arm across her shoulders. "Tony has finished for the day. Shall I order pizza? Then I will light the fire and you can fill me in."

"Sounds good to me."

So absorbed by the story in front of her, she kept reading, barely noticing Logan until she heard the crackling of the fire. The warmth only radiated from the fireplace a few feet, even with the heavy curtains drawn and the door shut.

As they munched on pizza, Paige took Logan through her information. She had drawn up a family tree and a timeline.

"See, Logan. Your great-grandfather was Thomas Hamilton, Sarah's brother. He died in the war. Apparently he had a very torrid affair with Ada Dunsford before he was deployed. Ada is the great-granddaughter of William Dunsford and his second wife, Gwendolyn Sealey, a widow. Ada and Thomas were sort of cousins a few times removed. "

"So William was married to Annie and when she left or died, he married Gwendolyn."

"Yes, but according to the dates in the family tree, William and Gwendolyn's first son was born before Annie died. This makes me think Gwendolyn was perhaps William's mistress. They married within weeks of Annie's death at sea, therefore making their baby son, Michael, legitimate."

"So, did they murder Annie?"

"Probably." She shivered then, partly from the chill and partly from the horrible thought of poor Annie's demise.

"Come closer to the fire. Tell me more about my great-grandparents and their love affair." He was already sitting on the shaggy rug by the hearth, his legs wide apart, his back resting on the old sideboard.

Paige settled between his legs and rested her back against his chest as he wrapped his arms around her waist. She opened Sarah's diary first and read several passages about her brother, Thomas, then she switched to Ada's diary. She read about their first meeting at a church dance and how they had danced the night away in each other's arms. Ada described Thomas as tall, dark, and handsome. The very next day he took her for a drive, and then to a concert and dinner.

They were passionately in love and consummated their relationship after the third date. It was easy for them to be together because Thomas owned a small house in town he had inherited from his godmother.

Logan stirred and wriggled his legs when Paige read out loud the passionate, uninhibited sexual encounters which Ada described in detail.

"Now I know where you get it from, Logan." She could feel the lump of his erection pressing against the top of her buttocks.

He laughed. "Maybe, but I think what a man really needs is to be madly in love with a responsive, sexy woman to get all fired up."

"And some sexy bedtime stories."

"Time for bed, my little ghost hunter." He lifted her to her feet, swept her into his arms, and carried her to the bed.

***

They were woken by heavy pounding on the door and Tony yelling for him to get his ass out of bed. It was almost morning break time. Logan groaned. He was warm and contented with his arms wrapped around Paige. His cock was hard and he wanted nothing more than to sink it into her pussy. He rubbed his erection against her butt and she pushed back against him before rolling over. He leant over and kissed her, his hands reaching for her breasts. They were rounded and supple, the nipples soft and pink. He took one in his mouth and sucked. It immediately hardened. Her hands cupped his balls and stroked his cock then with a shove, she pushed him onto his back. He was barely settled and she mounted him, sliding his throbbing cock into her pussy. It was hot and ready for him, so the moment his length slid in, he began to thrust. She clenched her pussy muscles tight around his cock and moved up and down to match his frantic rhythm. He knew he would feel guilty if she didn't come too but he just wanted a release. He looked up at her. She pouted a kiss as she squeezed her muscles hard on his throbbing cock.

"I can't wait, my love. Sorry."

She smiled. "I know. It's okay."

Her pussy clenched hard around his flesh, so it burned with the friction of her barely juiced pussy walls. His cock throbbed and pumped as his orgasm exploded through his balls and along his cock. He moaned as each spasm shook him and he thrust deep and hard. He felt his hot fluid squirt out into her pussy, filling it with creamy leavings. The last spasms had barely faded as he pulled her to him and kissed her hard.

"Thank you, my love."

Tony thumped on the door again and roared out something he was sure was crude in broken Italian. Logan cringed at its inference but

Paige just laughed as she rose above him to let his cock slide out of her. She rolled off him and snuggled back under the blankets.

"Go on. Get out there before poor Tony has an apoplexy."

***

Paige watched him roll out of bed and pull on his trunks and jeans. She admired his tight shapely ass and the defined sculpture of his muscular back. The scratches on his back had almost healed, but she noticed the dressing on his chest wounds was starting to loosen and made a mental note to replace it tonight.

Their hurried quickie had turned her on, but she hadn't quite made it to a climax. She lay quiet for a while after Logan left, but her body didn't calm. Running her hands over her body, she cupped her breasts and squeezed her nipples. Then she reached into her drawer, pulled out her big vibrator, and laid it beside her hip to warm a little. Idly she caressed her clit, thinking of Logan's cock thrusting into her. She loved the way it filled her, stretched her, and stroked every inch of her pussy. Sighing, Paige picked up the vibrator, turned it on to medium speed, and slid it deep into her pussy. She pulled it out and pushed it in again, raising her hips to meet its downward movement while at the same time, she caressed her clit, faster and faster.

It only took a few moments and she felt the familiar tingle. Today it was centered on her genitals, the inner lips puffing up with arousal, and her clit standing up stiff as she continued to rub and press it carefully against her pubic bone. The sensation erupted in her clit, spread through her pussy, and right up her torso making her buck against the vibrator as she buried it deep inside her, its trembling motion firing off sparks, and as the two sensations came together, her body shuddered its release.

With a passionate cry Paige flopped back on the bed, gasping for breath, and giving another couple of small groans as she left the vibrator in her pussy, the gentle purring of the device massaging the tension away. Finally, she pulled it out and her pussy collapsed into contented softness and she lay there her eyes closed, feeling the soft undulations of her climax aftershocks as they lapped slowly through her body.

Soothed and satiated, she dozed for a while then feeling guilty about lying in bed while everyone else worked, she climbed out and headed for the bathroom.

***

Logan looked up at her as she joined the men seated around the machinery, eating their lunch. She saw the question in his eyes and knew he was feeling guilty about not satisfying her this morning. She smiled and poked her tongue out, took a sandwich, and seated herself on the box beside him.

As she finished her first mouthful she leaned in and whispered almost silently in his ear, "Don't worry this girl has her ways and means." It was almost impossible to hold down the giggle at the color that tinted his cheeks and she wondered if the thought of her masturbating had hardened his cock. She suspected it had and she intended to exact her inch or two of flesh come evening.

They were just dispersing after lunch when Christine arrived.

As they showed her inside, Logan leaned close to her.

"Will you let me watch you next time?"

The heat rushed into her face at the thought of Logan watching her use her big vibrator—or even helping her use it. Her pussy tingled in anticipation, but that was slightly cooled by a sense of self consciousness. She had never masturbated in front of anyone before. She had never felt safe enough with anyone to reveal how she pleasured herself.

Once they were settled with coffee, Christine laid out her files. She had done heaps of work and lots of tests. She took a sculpture out of the large box she had brought with her. Paige gasped as she looked into the reconstructed face of Annie Dunsford. There was no mistaking the identity of the skeleton, and there was no way Annie had drowned at sea. Christine explained that Annie had a severe head injury caused by a blunt instrument and that this was the cause of her death. She also had statistics about her age, height, approximate weight, and combined with Paige's data and dates, they came to the conclusion that Annie had been killed two days after the birth of Dunsford's illegitimate son by Gwen Sealey, and that Dunsford and Sealey had married two weeks after her death. The DNA samples had proven that Paige and Logan were both descendants of Annie's.

"So, with all this information, we can prove that Annie was murdered and buried under the floor. But can we prove who actually did it?" Paige asked.

Christine flicked through the pages of her report. "Probably not, but if you take into account the diaries and what the older daughter wrote, I would guess that both of them would be complicit in the event. Gwen Sealey had the stronger motive—she didn't want to lose her son. What she wanted was a father and a name for her son. She could have that with Annie out of the picture."

Logan took Paige's hand and squeezed it. "I suppose it doesn't really matter which one did it, as long as Annie gets some form of justice and a last resting place. So what happens now?"

Christine started to pack her research up and handed Paige a second box. "This is copies of everything I've done. You can have this to keep. We can get the cause of death changed on the certificate as well. As for the skeleton, it should be interred, and because you are family, it is technically your responsibility. So do you have any preferences?"

"I think..." Logan began

"We should..." Paige said at the same moment.

They both stopped and Logan indicated Paige should continue.

"I think we should put her beside her great-great-granddaughter, Sarah Hamilton, in the local cemetery."

Logan smiled. "I agree. I think you will find her daughter, Elizabeth, is also buried there."

Christine put the last of the evidence away. "Then it's settled. I would like to attend, if that's okay?"

"That would be lovely, Christine."

After Christine left, Paige carefully packed the diaries away and put them under her bed.

Annie re-appeared as they were cooking dinner.

She stormed through the doorway, her face contorted into a twisted mask of rage. She screamed at them.

"It does matter. It does. It does. Where's my justice?"

Chapter Eight

P aige faced her, her hands held out. "Annie, calm down…"

The ghost screeched and waved her arms. Every loose item in the room stirred, rose into the air, and whirled around them. "I will have justice!"

"We can't do anymore," Paige informed her.

"I will have justice," the spirit of Annie wailed.

The doors of the old sideboard crashed open, then shut, the mirror on top shuddered, and cracked. The drawers flew open. All the contents flew out of the sideboard, crashing and smashing on the floor. All of Paige's documents scattered around the room and crockery crashed to the floor and against the walls, disintegrating into thousands of shards.

Then the specter advanced towards Logan, her hands outstretched.

"I should have finished you off years before, killer's spawn."

Paige leapt across the room just in time to come between them. "Stop, Annie. Stop! Hurting Logan is not the answer."

The apparition halted its forward charge.

"I will have justice." The fire tending tools clattered and rose into the air. The metal weapons circled above them. "Move, Daughter. The murderer's spawn must die."

The items whizzed close to their heads.

"No," Paige shouted.

"Then you shall die at his side," the ghost screamed.

The shovel hit Logan in the shoulder. He yelped. The fire dog crashed against the back of Paige's knee, and she slumped to the floor as her leg collapsed under the force of the blow. Even as Logan tried to hold her up, the coal brush caught him across the head. He cried out. The air was full of flying objects, swirling around and around them.

"Get under the table, Paige." He grabbed her by the waist and hauled her with him, as he staggered to retreat under the onslaught. They backed in under the table and huddled in the furthest corner. They heard Cat yowl from on top of the table. Logan tried to protect Paige from the worst of the attack, and the table shuddered under the force of the items that slammed against it. The lights flickered and went out. Only the glow from the fire and the silver outline from the marauding specter lit the room.

"Die." There was a hiss and a whoosh and the air was full of glowing embers, soot, and ash. They swirled like shooting stars onto the curtains, the sideboard, the carpet, and the table top. Small flames ignited. Red licking fingers of flame crawled up the curtains. The carpet smoldered from a hundred little fires. Toxic smoke rose.

Paige coughed.

Logan gasped for air.

"Die."

The curtains burst into flames.

"Oh my God, she intends to burn us alive!" Paige shrieked.

The fire was already between them and the door, and the burning curtains framed the only window. Paige felt sick. She couldn't breathe, so she got down as low as she could. Unidentified items continued to thud on the table top. Behind her, Logan was coughing as he struggled to speak to the operator of triple zero.

Then she remembered the small fire extinguisher they kept by the gas stove for safety.

"Stay here." Paige crawled on her belly the two feet it needed to close her hand around the small appliance. In one smooth movement, she rolled over, stood up, and pulled the pin. White foam roared out of the spout. She smothered the flames on the carpet between her and the table then attacked the remnants of the curtains blazing at the window. Then Logan was beside her, using the mat from in front of the fireplace to smother the flames eating the table.

Cat sat pressed up against the wall, his eyes wide with terror as he spat and growled.

As they could hear the sirens screaming towards them, Logan turned, pushed up the window, and pushed Paige over the window ledge, even as she still clung to the extinguisher, trying to smother the nearest flames. He swept the mat over Cat and dragged the poor terrorized animal, screeching against his chest, as he followed Paige out the window. As their feet hit the ground, the fire engine jerked to halt just inches from them.

There was a spine-chilling scream, and they could see Annie outlined by the flames that leapt up behind her. Then the hoses sprayed water into the room and she dissolved.

Cat wriggled free, and raced away, his tail dragging behind him. Within thirty minutes, the fire was out.

Paige turned and pulled Logan into a passionate embrace.

He kissed her hard.

She kissed him back with a desperate fierceness. "I thought we were going to die," she whimpered.

He tightened his embrace. "Me too," he whispered.

It was almost midnight by the time they had finished with the paramedics, the firemen, and the police. On advice they didn't need, they collected some clothes and found themselves a motel room for the night.

***

The ring of the phone dragged them both from sleep before breakfast, and so began a round of tedious tasks—firstly the police, then the insurance, then Tony, and the local paper. They were tired and frustrated by the time they shut the motel door behind them after dinner.

Paige slumped into the chair and Logan disappeared into the en-suite. She heard water running then Logan appeared in the doorway, stark naked. His cock was hanging flaccid over his balls and he stood there silently to allow her to study him closely. His long legs were slightly apart and his hips angled slightly towards her in a daring stance of offering. He flexed his muscles and the pecs contracted slightly. She dropped her gaze back down to his cock. It was already moving, thickening and hardening.

Logan gave a lazy smile, letting his cock respond to her gaze, while his hands rested on his slim hips. "The spa is filling—far too much water for one person," he drawled.

"Really."

"Yep, and I would make it worth your while." He slid his hands down his hips and onto his thighs then proceeded to firstly cup his balls then to cradle his semi-hard cock. He lifted it, stroked it then squeezed the head to milk the pre-cum into a glistening pool in the eye.

With the tip of her tongue she wet her dry lips. Already her pussy was aching with desire and she intended to make the most of the anticipation. She stood and began a slow strip tease, undoing each button on her shirt, one at a time. Then she slipped it off her shoulders and let it drop to the floor. His cock immediately danced in response. With nimble fingers she unclipped her bra and slowly let it slide down over the swell of her breasts, but she paused fractionally before she exposed her nipples, and then took one step forward. His cock jumped again.

Finally she let her bra fall away to expose herself fully then she reached for her jeans button. Just before she stepped forward again, she pushed the tight fitting denim over her hips seductively, swaying to ease the passage of the encasing material. Curving her body into a tempting pose she stood there in front of him in only her lacy G-string. Logan's cock was almost fully erect, and she could see the uneven rise and fall of his chest from his agitated breathing. His gaze was locked onto her naked body. Teasing him with a sexy, suggestive smile she stepped right up to him.

In silent worship of his masculinity, she knelt down in front of him and flicked her tongue over his head, tasting the salty tang of his pre-cum, and she heard his indrawn breath whistle in his chest. Grasping his shaft in a firm grip she brought her mouth down to engulf his head. At first she sucked just the tip, running her tongue under the edge of his knob. Then sliding her hand towards the base of his cock, she engulfed the whole shaft in her mouth. He moaned. She sucked. The taste of him was intoxicating; warm male cock, pre-cum, and the scent of soap and aftershave filled her nostrils.

With her free hand she cupped his balls and gently squeezed each testicle. Moving on she felt the tickle of pubic hair against her hand as she slid it between his legs and caressed his butt. He moaned again as he reached down to grasp her shoulders and lift her from the floor. As she rose, she let his hard throbbing cock slip from her mouth. He kissed her hard, his flavor the spice heating the arousal between them before he scooped her up into his arms and carried her to the spa.

The water was almost to the top and the surface was covered in fragrant bubbles. Logan lowered her into the water, turned the taps off and then climbed in with her, making the water slosh over the edge to flood the en-suite floor.

"Ooops." Logan grinned as he looked over the edge with a rueful smile.

Paige giggled because he didn't look in the slightest bit repentant as he turned on the jets and forcing more water out of the tub and onto the floor. For a long moment they both luxuriated in the turbulent bubbles. Paige had her eyes closed, feeling safe and peaceful for the first time in a long while, and then Logan was caressing her body with a cake of silky soap—sliding it over her shoulders, down her arms, and back up, before moving down her cleavage and over her breasts. He soaped each breast and circled her nipples. Then he moved down, soaping and caressing every inch of her body, right down to her toes, before he took hold of her waist and turned her around so her back was pressed up against his chest.

She could feel his erection as he lifted each of her legs up and laid them over his long muscular ones, opening up her pussy. With a light touch he caressed her body, thighs, and breasts then slid both hands between her legs. Logan agitated the water near the entrance to her pussy and the turbulence caressed her tender flesh. Stroking her clit, he drew it out between thumb and finger, making Paige moan as her whole body throbbed in the combined effects of warm bubbling water and his body pressed against hers while his hands skillfully played with her sensitive inner lips and clit. Logan then grasped her hips and lifted her almost out of the water to accommodate his throbbing cock that stood stiff and tall in his groin.

As he lowered her, she guided his cock into her entrance. She sighed as she sank down, engulfing his whole length. When she was settled on him, he thrust with small fast motions. She semi-floated in the water, and he grabbed her hips and pulled her down each time to meet his upward thrusts, spreading the sensation through her body from the top of her head to deep inside. She closed her legs then and tightened her grip on his cock, making his thrusts feel harder as they jammed into her clenched pussy.

He groaned in response. "Oh God, Paige, that feels so good."

Her pussy muscles clenched, then relaxed, then clenched again, and without warning, her climax burst around his cock and raced through her body. She arched back against his chest and cried out as she was swamped by waves of sensation, and his faster, shallower, action magnified the release. As she sensed his inevitable climax, she spread her legs to accommodate his need to sink deep into her. He groaned a deep gut wrenching groan that ended on a gasp of air. He wrapped his hands around her and laid his head against her back and she could feel his body shuddering as he struggled to regain control. They sat in silence for a time, pressed together, his cock still crammed inside her pussy.

The water was cooling when she reluctantly eased herself from his lap.

Later, as they lay cuddled together under the heavy motel quilt waiting for sleep to find them, Logan suddenly sighed and spoke.

"What now, my love? The fire was the last straw, especially when she was happy to hurt you. I don't think I can do this much more."

"Me either. I thought we had given her what she wanted. I thought it would be over."

"Yes, so did I, but obviously she wants her killer named specifically."

"So how do we do that? We know it's either William Dunsford or Gwen Sealey."

"I don't know, my love, but I'm too tired to care tonight."

***

All the next day, mournful sobbing pulsed right through the house. The plumber didn't believe it was the wind through the cracks by the windows, but kept working under duress. Tony was finished, but when the stone mason turned up to check out the job, he asked Logan what that bloody awful noise was. There was little to salvage from the fire-ravaged room and the chaos from Annie's temper tantrum. Everything was either burned or waterlogged.

Paige happily handed over to the clean-up team and headed into town.

Christine looked up as she entered her office. "What can I do for you?"

"Can I get a copy of all those documents and your report please? We had a fire at the house and everything is damaged."

Christine frowned. "Of course you can, but how did the fire start?"

"I'm not sure... well, there was some sort of explosion in the fire-place and embers spread around the room. It was alight before we could do anything."

"That's not good. You and Logan could have been killed."

Paige nodded. "Christine, as I haven't read your report, could you tell me if there was anything in it that would further identify the killer. I know it has to be either William Dunsford or his mistress, Gwen Sealey."

"Does it matter that much? The crime is almost one hundred and fifty years old."

Paige nodded. "It's important."

"Well, the evidence showed she was hit over the head several times with a blunt object that split her skull open just behind the ear. This indicates that she was hit by someone about the same height as her and I suspect from the blow that it was done by a left-handed person, as it came in slightly from the front. I believe it took several blows to break the skull and they were administered either by a weaker person or someone under the influence of drink. Does that help?"

Christine's assistant brought the photocopies to her, and Paige spread them on the desk until she found what she was looking for—a photo of an elderly William sitting at a desk. He was signing a document. Behind him stood his wife, Gwen, a shortish, dumpy woman. She slapped the photos on the desk for Christine to look at. "Look. Gwen has to be the murderer."

"I would agree and I believe you said she'd just had a baby, so that would account for her lack of strength."

Paige snatched up the papers. "Thanks Christine. You're a gem. Have to go and tell Logan."

***

"Logan, Logan. Where are you? I have some more information."

Logan emerged from the new master bedroom. He was shirtless, his jeans hung low down on his slim hips, and he was covered in dust.

"Where's the fire?"

Paige stopped and stared at him. "That's not funny."

They stared at each other for a long moment then Logan realized just what he'd said. They both burst into laughter.

Logan recovered first. "So what's so important?" He stepped forward and gave her tentative kiss on the cheek, trying to spare her the worst of the dust.

"I know who killed Annie—for certain. It was Gwen."

"How can you be so sure?"

"Christine confirmed the killer was left-handed and shorter than Annie and look, I have these photos. See William. He's signing a document—with his right hand. And here you can see he would have been around six foot tall. And look, Gwen is fanning herself using her left hand. She would have been shorter than Annie too. Gwen is the killer."

"My God, that is why she hates me—Gwendolyn Sealey is my direct ancestor. I'm the offspring of her killer. She probably thought I was Michael, the illegitimate child she was killed for."

"Yes, and the house was put in trust by Annie's guardian to protect her. Annie never actually owned it, so William or his descendants from Gwen could not inherit it. That explains why it went to Margaret after Elizabeth died so young. Annie does not want you to inherit the house because you are Gwen's descendant. She doesn't know about Ada and Thomas. She has trouble with time too."

Logan grabbed her in a huge bear hug.

"You're a genius, my love." He kissed her hard then pulled back. "So, what now?"

"Somehow we have to convince Annie that she has justice and that it is okay for you to inherit the house. Then maybe we can lay her to rest."

"No more haunting?"

The sobbing continued, unabated, but the ghost did not appear until it was almost dark outside. Then she seemed to be keeping her distance as she hovered on the edge of the glow thrown by the globe.

"Annie," Paige said quietly.

Logan came up close behind Paige and wrapped his arms around her waist.

The apparition wailed as she clutched her hands to her breast. "I am desecrated—driven to rage by injustice, Daughter, and still the killer's spawn contaminates my house."

"You shouldn't have tried to harm us."

"I cannot rest without justice. Must have justice."

"But harming us is not how to get it."

"He is the killer's spawn."

"He is also your descendent, Annie. Your great-grandson, Thomas Hamilton, loved Ada Dunsford, William and Gwen's great-great-granddaughter. Ada and Thomas had one child before Thomas was killed in the war. That child, Marcus Dunsford-Hamilton was Logan's great-great-grandfather."

The misty face of the spirit contorted. "Noooo," she wailed. "My child carries the blood of the damned. No, it cannot be." The specter wobbled and faded, then disappeared for a moment then reappeared, more solid than ever. Now she covered her face with her hands. "So much time I have lain in that cold hole without mourning and without justice. So many have been and gone and my own children, dead so long ago. There is no justice."

"Yes, Annie, you have been dead for around one hundred and seventy years. Your killer has been dead for around about one hundred and fifty years. We cannot exact justice. We cannot have her convicted. It's too late."

Annie wailed again. "All this angst and still there is no justice. Can I never rest?"

Logan stepped out from behind Paige and moved towards the apparition. She continued to wail.

"Annie, shush for a moment. Listen to me."

"You have her blood in your veins, Why should I listen to you, killer's spawn?"

"You should listen because I also have your blood in my veins."

Annie stopped wailing and stared at Logan, her hands clenched in front of her.

"Annie, my ancestor, Gwendolyn Sealey, was wrong to become your husband's mistress, wrong to have his child, and very wrong—evil, in fact—to murder you as she did. I can't even say she did it because she loved him. She did it for her personal gain and the security of her child. You have been wronged, Annie—very wronged—but so was she, by your husband, William."

"We have proof that Gwen murdered you, and that will be recorded in the family history. Murder will be recorded on your death certificate, changed from 'lost at sea'." Paige held out her hands to the specter. "Can you accept what little we can do, Annie? Can it be enough justice?"

Annie glared at them. "You call that justice. And all the time, he"—she pointed at Logan—"he gets my house—my house with his tainted blood."

"We get the house, Annie. He and I, together."

"No, only you, Daughter. Never the killer's spawn. Never." She charged at Logan, her hands outstretched, her face a twisted mask of hatred.

Before either of them could react, the ghost had Logan pinned against the wall, squashing him, suffocating him with her evil-filled translucence. He pushed vainly against the force but was helpless to free himself.

Paige snatched up a large umbrella from the hat rack and waved it at the apparition. She struck it on the head, her weapon sliding through the misty apparition.

"Leave him be, Annie. Back off."

Logan coughed and gasped as he struggled to get air into his lungs.

Paige was desperate. She beat the ghost again and again, and finally the specter of her great-great-grandmother turned towards her. Without waiting for a response from the ghostly figure, Paige rammed the spike of the umbrella into the misty figure.

"You are dead, Annie. Go now from this place. You have all we can give. Go," she screamed, as she stabbed again and again at the misty shape before her.

The apparition began to fade. "I will have justice. He will go," she screeched, before she faded completely.

And she was gone. The house felt cold and empty somehow, as if it had the soul ripped out of it. Paige shivered and Logan embraced her.

"Is it over, my love? Will she rest now?"

Paige sighed. "I don't think so. She wants you dead—she has always wanted you dead."

"Maybe when we lay her to rest, it might be over. I hope so."

"It's sad. She's waited for so long."

He looked down at her and brushed her fringe back from her face. First, he lightly kissed her nose, then her brow, before her took command of her mouth, devouring the soft flesh until she could hardly breathe. Only then did he pull away.

"Well, we will just have to build a new soul for the house. Give it a new life. Maybe one day it might have a family at its center.

"A family?" Her response was almost a squeal.

"Yes, Paige, a family. This is a family home, but it is also our home. If we can lay Annie to rest, will you stay here with me and build a family? A Dunsford-Hamilton family—a happy loving family with lots of kids? A story to overwrite the sadness of the past."

"But I thought..."

He put his finger on her lips. "Don't think, just reply."

"Oh Logan, I would really like to spend the rest of my life with you, building a family... but what if we can't get rid of Annie? She will always be trying to kill you."

He cut her words off as he took command of her mouth again and proceeded to overwhelm her with a hard, demanding kiss.

"Then this is what we will do—you and I, if we cannot get rid of the vengeful ghost, we will move somewhere else."

***

Two days later, just before they went to the cemetery to bury Annie's remains, they returned to the house. They went hand in hand. The house felt cold and empty. They stood silently in the hallway and waited.

Paige looked around, hoping the apparition would appear.

"Annie, we have come to talk to you. To say what needs to be said..." A cold breeze whispered along her skin. "I know you're here, Annie, so I will just say what I have come to say. We are going to the cemetery now to inter your bodily remains in consecrated ground. After that, I expect you to be gone from this place. This time is ours—yours is long past."

The ghost appeared through the lounge room door.

"You and the killer's spawn seek to take my home from me—to cast me out in the cold..." She swept the coat stand over, spilling the contents at Paige's feet. "Never." She approached and stood nose to nose with Paige, her hands on her hips, her face a vision of anger and pain.

Paige refused to back down. She felt Logan squeeze her hand tightly and she squeezed back. It was now or never.

She glared at the spirit of her ancestor. "This is how it is, Annie. Either you move on or Logan and I will sell this house—your house—to strangers. Do you hear me? To strangers. We will move far away. I will never return to this house..."

"No, Daughter, this house is yours. To live in it was always your destiny."

"I will make a new destiny, Annie. I will not suffer you hurting Logan—do you hear? I will sell your house to strangers. Then again, I might even demolish it..."

The apparition wailed and screeched as she swung away from Paige.

"No, no, no. You cannot."

Paige stepped forward until she was almost touching the specter. "You cannot stop me, Annie. I will demolish it. Do you hear me? It will be no more than a pile of rubble. Do you understand? A pile of rubble."

The apparition turned. Tears were flowing down her misty cheeks. She wrung her hands then reached out to Paige. "Please, Daughter, do not destroy what is yours. Please don't. I will go if this is what you wish." She wailed as she dissolved into the gloom of the house.

***

Two hours later they laid Annie to rest between her great-great-grand-daughter, Sarah, and her oldest child. There were only four of them at the graveside—Paige, Logan, Christine, and the lawyer, Martin Atkins, who came out of respect for Sarah Hamilton. Paige laid a red rose on the white coffin beside the wreath of yellow roses. Logan held her hand as tears suddenly filled her eyes. It was almost like saying a final goodbye to a friend—a difficult, challenging, but special, friend. They lingered for a while at the graveside after the others had left.

"She can rest now."

"She can."

***

He watched Paige as they drove back to the house after dinner. She laid her head back on the headrest and closed her eyes. He had not planned to fall in love again. The last time had been a hard lesson learned—his new wife declaring after their wedding that she didn't actually want children and intended to get on the board of directors of his company. But that was nothing to the fact she had been secretly buying up shares until she had slightly more than fifty per cent and was embezzling money with the help of his accountant, who had become her lover. He had been forced to strip the company of the remaining assets. It had been a bitter battle.

It had shocked him to find himself falling head over heels in love with this willowy blonde, even as he'd resented her having any control over the direction his life would take. Now he was smitten.

She stirred when he pulled up at the house. "Oh, I thought you would want to go back to the hotel."

"Wouldn't you rather be here in our home?"

She sat up. "Yes but..."

"Paige, I don't think Annie will be any risk now, even if she's still haunting the house. I think she will be too afraid of your threat to do anything."

Paige leaned toward him and pressed her lips to his. She tasted of warm sweetness, coffee and peppermint. A sense of protectiveness flared inside. He wanted to protect her, and knew instinctively that would be a challenge, for this woman he loved was feisty, strong, and determined.

They found a very subdued Cat sitting on the door mat. They hadn't seen him since the fire, but he seemed pleased to see them, both of them, and he purred as he followed them inside. The house was cold and dark, so Logan switched on the lights and turned the small portable heater on in their bedroom while Paige made them hot chocolate. They piled into bed and with the pillows piled up behind them, and the duvet up to their chins, they snuggled together and drank their hot chocolate after sharing the pink marshmallows melting in the creamy liquid.

The room was warmer now and he leaned over her as she lay cuddled up in the duvet. He gently touched her breasts and played almost absently with her nipples. They became erect almost immediately, but he didn't follow through with more caressing. He wanted Paige to do something special for him tonight and he wanted her to do it willingly—trustingly. He needed her to want to. He leaned down and kissed her now, a lingering kiss that tasted of milky chocolate. She reached up and pulled him on top of her. His cock was already getting hard, but tonight he was in no hurry to use his erection.

"My love, you remember the other morning... when I left you unsatisfied, and you said you had ways and means...?"

"Yes."

"Would you show me... your ways and means?" He saw the blush color her cheeks. "You don't have to, love, if you're not comfortable. I just thought it would be nice..."

"Oh Logan, I have never masturbated in front of anyone before. It's not that I don't want to share with you..."

"Just do what you feel comfortable with or we can leave it. It's not that important."

She giggled. "Somehow I think it is. Maybe it is a big turn on for you?"

He shook his head. "I don't know, my love, for I have never had a woman pleasure herself for me before, but thinking about it has made me hard as hell."

She reached down between them and enclosed his throbbing cock in her hand and stroked up and down the length a few times before she pushed him off her, then rolled over and fished out her vibrator. As she pressed it against her side she lay flat on her back, and began to stroke her breasts; he almost exploded right then and there. He watched as she cupped them, massaged them softly then firmer before she took her nipples between finger and thumb and rolled and tugged them until they rose out of the dark areola like little light houses. Then she massaged her breasts with the palms of her hands before sliding them down over her rib cage and slightly rounded stomach. With both hands she covered her naked mound, and squeezed her lips together before sliding her hands down either side until her fingers met just above her butt hole.

With a delicate caress she then slid both hands up between her lips, her fingers buried in the dark, damp, fleshy layers. She watched him as she parted her legs and gave a small smile as Logan moved slightly so he could see. It was almost unbearable to sit and watch, because all he wanted was to jump her and sink his painfully hard cock into her flesh. Then she opened herself up so he could see right inside as her fingers caressed the lips with gentle strokes. He could see the entrance to her pussy, a small indentation of flesh that was glistening with fluid.

He watched in fascination as she slid her hands past her entrance and eased her mound up so he could see the slightly darker pink of her clit as it poked its tiny round head up out of the swollen flesh surrounding it. She played with her clit, running her finger around its base then taking it between finger and thumb and stroking it in the same way she stroked his cock.

His cock danced and ached. Still, he didn't move or touch. Logan just sat there and watched her erotic display in awe. He groaned when he saw her slip two fingers inside herself, making the fluid squelch out of her pussy as she thrust them in and out. Oh God, he so wanted to do that. Almost panting with arousal, he tore his gaze away to look at her face.

She watched him, watch her. That almost flipped him over the edge. Still holding her lips apart, she picked up the big vibrator, turned it on, and after rubbing up and down her lips to lubricate it, she held it at her entrance, paused for a moment before she slid it ever so slowly in—just a small amount. Just the knob. Then she withdrew it and then thrust again, deep this time.

She moaned as she thrust it in and out. Logan could not bear it any longer. He reached out and placed his hand over hers as she manipulated the device. For a while he was guided by her pace, but then she pulled her hand away and he inserted the vibrator then pulled it out, again and again, while she was still rubbing her clit. With his other hand he caressed below her pussy right round to her butt.

Paige arched her back and cried out as he kept thrusting, then bucked her hips to match his movement. She was gasping and whimpering. He saw her pussy flush and swell and her muscles clenched the vibrator as she climaxed. The slightest touch of her hand stayed his movement and he let the vibrator slip out of her. As he watched she massaged the area slowly with her hand, giving a slight moan now and again before she lay still.

Moments later she opened her eyes and looked directly up at him.

"Make love to me, Logan."

He didn't need to be asked twice. He slid over her and with her guidance, he slipped into her pussy. He glided in and out and she met his thrusts. He thought he would explode right then and he tried to hold back because he wanted her to come again. She reached down and rubbed her clit and he felt her tighten around his cock. She arched beneath him, tilting her head back as she gasped for breath, her second climax gripping his cock. It burned and throbbed deep inside her hot, wet flesh and he felt the rush of sensation as he came with a thunderous climax. Three thrusts later and they both collapsed in a sweaty pile, totally satiated. Logan rolled off her and pulled her back against his chest. He was still struggling to steady his breathing.

"Oh my God, Paige, you're so beautiful. I love you."

"I love you too, Logan."

"I have never been so turned on as I was when you were pleasuring yourself. Thank you my love, for your gift."

"Gift?"

"Yes for loving and trusting me enough to allow yourself to be so vulnerable."

"I do trust you, Logan. With you, I feel safe to be me."

"Do you trust me enough to become my wife? To have my children? To make a family with me?"

"Yes."

His body ached with anticipation of the future they would build, even as his mind tried to grapple with the shock of what he had done. He had asked her to be his wife. Good grief, he was smitten. But then, she had agreed. That didn't surprise him as much as the fact that she had willingly shared her most private act with him—had made herself so vulnerable and in doing so, captured his heart in a way it had never been touched before. He held her until she slept. Then in the intimate silence of the darkness, he heard a soft whisper.

"And so, they will forge their own great love story."

He listened harder, but there was nothing, and he allowed himself to be lulled to sleep in the warmth of his lover's embrace.

THE END.

About the author

Dionie was a closet writer for several years before she got brave enough to share her work with anyone. After she joined Eyre Writers Inc, a creative writing group in the seaside town of Port Lincoln she really began to improve.

Her first book was a 100,000 words family saga, but after a workshop on 'How to write a Mills and Boon', she embarked on a new direction—writing the romance novel.

After being made redundant from the job she loved in 2011 she became a carer for her frail, vision-impaired mother and turned to fulfilling her dream of becoming a published author.

Because she has a very eclectic nature she was unable to choose just one genre – hence she writes Young Adult as Dionie McNair, Fantasy as Emily Tyler and Romance with a bit of spice and a touch of a twist as Cassandra Hawke and Thrillers/crime as DL McNair.

When Dionie is not writing she enjoys spending time with family and friends, especially her mother, three wonderful adult children and adorable grandchildren. She also enjoys egg decorating and carving, reading, of course, painting, cooking, swimming and target archery.

Visit her at Home | Dionie McNair

Also by this
Author

<u>***Young Adult: writing as Dionie McNair***</u>

FINDING THE UPSDIE OF DOWN. (stand alone)
Broken by bullying Tabitha volunteers and finds just what she needs
to mend her broken life.
Being bullied has always been a part of Tabitha Cockell's life. Her
tormentor Amelia has hounded her since first grade with cruel taunts
and name-calling and nasty rumors both face-to-face and online. She
attempts suicide but is saved by the guy she has just started dating after
he reads her suicide note on Face book.

Survival means she has to face life, but she doesn't know how until she sees a crew of State Emergency Service volunteers at work. She finds the courage to join and her decision soon has her seeing and understanding life from a whole new perspective.

***

The Abrasaxon's Daughter Series

Re-release pending
Book 1: THE SCORPION'S HEART
Book 2: CURSE OF THE CHAKKA CHAKKA
New releases 2026
Book 3: ILLUSIONS OF WAR
Book 4: THE LOST ARCHON

Watch for these great fantasy Young Adult books

Adult Fantasy: writing as Emily Tyler

Thrones of Annaticcia series

Book 1: TWIN BETRAYAL

Princess Rosin, legitimate only daughter of the royal Bond of Le Chéile is destined to be Queen of Keswin but her twin, Ciara covets the crown. Her lover, Lord Devon also wants the crown and he seizes it in a bloody coup.

While fleeing to safety, Rosin saves and falls in love with a wounded soldier, Arlan, and when no noble will offer a bond, she becomes determined to form a Bond of Le Chéile the man she loves.

But Rosin knows she must soon put their potential happiness aside and return and save her throne.

***

Dykarin Dragon Shifters

Book 1 ANARCHY

Taminisha, Regent of Aikanshin is broken and dying from Nyket's savage attack, but she must survive to fulfil her destiny and save Dykarin from the Era of Darkness.

Death and grief stalk her. Love a peace are transient gifts in the midst of Nyket's tyranny.

Already stripped of all that matters Taminisha's will to live is crushed when Nyket cruelly uses her body to breed and heir.

Nyket snatches the newborn from her breast and tries to kill Taminisha. But she escapes with the help of Khoury and the mysterious child Kashwen.

Gravley injured she crash lands on Oventi Island, and stalked from above by Nyket, she begs Spirit to take her hand end her misery.

***

Dykarin Dragon Shifters

Book 2 SANCTUARY

When Taminisha crash lands on Oventi she finds sanctuary instead of
death with Khimaera outcasts and the three Siblings.

But that security is threatened as Nyket continues to ravage Dykarin
but resistance against him is building.

Rabikan falls to Nyket as Adakan rescues his soulmate Jycosa and flees
back to the sanctuary of Mitikan, the only clan still free of the scourge
of Nyket.

In Mitikan with Guardian Okeyon's assistance Larkin rallies the Khimaera, refugees and surviving Ellkiiyn to train and prepare for a final
battle against Nyket.

Tarlitek brings Jabrikan, the young heir apparent to Aikanshin, out of
hiding to lead all Ellkiiyn to freedom and restore the true Guardians
of the Clans and kill Nyket. The fight is no longer about equality but
subjugation.

Erotic Romance: writing as Cassandra Hawke

BLOOD TIES A BROKEN HEART (stand alone)

When Rylee returns to Adelaide to take over her Godmother's stables, seeing Ashford St Clair brings back memories of past events—when he'd sacrificed his promising equestrian career and alienated Rylee in the process.

Ash is determined to win Rylee back and they reach an uneasy compromise when their passion for each other is re-ignited

But the deeds of the past still haunt the present threatening their relationship. An old enemy returns to cause trouble for Rylee—Ash's sister, Arden—the one who brought about Ash's downfall in the first place. She makes it clear that there is no room for Rylee in Ash's life and she'll do anything to make sure the lovers remain apart.

Will Rylee come to terms with the mistakes she and Ash made in the past and learn to love and trust each other again?

***

DEMOLITION OF THE HEART (stand alone)

Kayla Mackenzie id shocked when she finds out the man she has just made passionate love to is responsible for her priceless paintings being in a charity auction and intends to demolish her beloved family home. Wade has no idea that his inheritance of historical Ainsley House has been carefully orchestrated and that he is a pawn in a complex plot that will not only deprive Kayla of her beloved family home and her inheritance, but also her life. The thing he hadn't counted on was the impetus and fiery-tempered Kayla stealing his well-guarded heart before he even knew it was at risk.

Their confrontations are fierce and explosive and they both determinedly maintain joint residence of the historic house, but they find themselves fighting an entirely different battle as the smoldering attraction between them erupts into an inferno of desire and sexual attraction.

They final get to the truth of how the house came to be in Wade's hands and Kayla claims her inheritance and strikes a business deal with Wade that will save the house.

***

CULTIVATE A LOVE MATCH (stand alone)

Her love heals his broken heart. Can his heal hers?

When lawyer Blake Gifford comes to re-claim his block of land from the guerrilla gardener's explosive chemistry sparks between him and their leader, Tya. She breached his carefully built walls and taught his heart to love again with one close encounter. But Tya comes from the wrong side of the tracks and believes she is not worthy of any good man's love.

Six months earlier Blake jilted his unfaithful fiancé Stephanie at the altar. Now she claims he's the father of her unborn child and wants them to be a family. Is the baby his? Will it make a difference to how he feels? Is their love enough to vanquish the specter of Tya's upbringing marred by prostitution, drugs, assault.

www.ingramcontent.com/pod-product-compliance
Lightning Source LLC
Chambersburg PA
CBHW070957180726

48291CB00004B/1331